I0641037

Osgood Field

The Fields of Sowerby near Halifax, England, and of Flushing, New York

with some notices of the families of Underhill, Bowne, Burling, Hazard, and Osgood

Osgood Field

The Fields of Sowerby near Halifax, England, and of Flushing, New York
with some notices of the families of Underhill, Bowne, Burling, Hazard, and Osgood

ISBN/EAN: 9783337381073

Printed in Europe, USA, Canada, Australia, Japan

Cover: Foto ©Andreas Hilbeck / pixelio.de

More available books at **www.hansebooks.com**

The Fields of Sowerby

NEAR HALIFAX, ENGLAND, AND OF

FLUSHING, NEW YORK

WITH SOME NOTICES OF THE FAMILIES OF

UNDERHILL, BOWNE, BURLING, HAZARD, AND

OSGOOD

BY OSGOOD FIELD

FELLOW OF THE SOCIETY OF ANTIQUARIES OF LONDON, CORRESPONDING
MEMBER OF THE NEW ENGLAND HISTORIC GENEALOGICAL
SOCIETY AND THE NEW YORK GENEALOGICAL
AND BIOGRAPHICAL SOCIETY, ETC.

LONDON

PRINTED FOR PRIVATE CIRCULATION ONLY

1895

PREFACE.

HE family, to which this book relates, is a
very old one, as only in rare instances can
an unbroken descent from father to son be
traced, on indisputable documentary evidence,
for more than 600 years.

The author cannot claim that it has ever been greatly
distinguished ; or held a very high position. On the
other hand, the status of its members has always been
respectable, and their marriages have been contracted
with the best people of their respective neighbourhoods.
From the commencement of this history, they have
lived independently on their own land, although their
estates were sometimes small.

In the course of a life, which has extended beyond
the usual term, the author has collected much information relating to the family, and, in almost every case,
from original sources. The facts which he has gotten
together are mostly contained in loose memoranda,
which have never been arranged systematically, and
which will probably be scattered or destroyed after his
death. Every year the task of compiling a family history
becomes more difficult, owing to the loss or destruction
of ancient documents.

For these reasons, he has thought it well to put the more important materials he has gathered in such a shape, that those interested in these family matters who survive, or come after him, may have the benefit of his researches.

Beyond all, the author has endeavoured to be accurate, and he has quoted freely from the original documents.

He has not attempted to give all the later descendants of Robert Field, the patentee of Flushing; but it will be a comparatively easy task for those of them, who are now living, to trace their descent from his grandchildren or great-grandchildren, who are given as fully as the author could ascertain them.

In almost all cases he has followed the old records in their mode of spelling proper names, and he would remark here, that there was rarely any settled form of orthography for these before the middle of the seventeenth century. As an instance, the family name of John Field, the astronomer, is spelt three different ways in his " Ephemerides," published in 1558, although it is a small volume.

The Heaton branch has adhered to the spelling " Feild," which was, perhaps, the most common in the latter half of the sixteenth and first half of the seventeenth centuries.

The author has many extracts from old records and memoranda relating to other families of the same name, and had proposed to include the most interesting of these in this volume ; but owing to his absence, for several months, from the place where his papers are, the carrying out of this plan would delay the publication of this book longer than he thinks desirable.

The rolls of the Manor of Wakefield have thrown much light on the early history of the Fields residing there. An examination of these documents has shown that some suggestions, relating to the family, made by the author, before he knew of the existence of these ancient records, were erroneous.

PALAZZO COLONNA, ROME,
February 22nd, 1895.

THE FIELDS OF SOWERBY.

HE family name of Field is one of several, such as Wood, Hill, etc., derived from locality. Persons with corresponding patronymics may be found in every civilized country. The word originally signified land on which the timber had been felled, as distinguished from woodland. It is evident from the nature of its origin that there are many distinct families of the name, in no way related to each other, except in such manner as all mankind are supposed to be, from having two common ancestors.

It was anciently written Feld, or Felde, as was also the noun from which the name was derived ; but about the middle of the sixteenth century the spelling of both was changed to Field, or, in some cases, Feild. We find, for instance, in the early editions of the bible the well-known words printed thus, " consider the lilies of the *feld.*" The fact of the name being hereditary in the family to which this book relates as early as the middle of the thirteenth century, and probably at a still more remote period, indicates a so-called Norman origin.[1]

Burke states in one edition of his "Landed Gentry," under the head of De la Field,[2] that this family was originally in Alsace, where it was seated at the Chateau de la Feld, near Colmar, from the darkest period of the middle ages; that Hubertus de la Feld held lands in Lancashire in the 3rd of William I., and presumably accompanied the Conqueror to England; also that others of the name were proprietors of land in the same county in the twelfth and thirteenth centuries.

We have no authentic record of the companions of the Conqueror, and it is generally admitted by competent genealogists that the "roll of Battle Abbey" is imperfect, and has been tampered with. It does not, therefore, help us in this matter. Burke is not always reliable, and when the author wrote to him for his authority for the statements in his book, he replied that he had forgotten where he had found them, or from whom he received them. The author has not often met with the name in England prior to the middle of the thirteenth century. In the great roll of the Pipe there is mention of a Hugo de la Felde under the head of the Counties of Bucks and Beds, in the 1st of Richard I.

---

[1] Freeman says in his history of the Norman Conquest that there is no well ascertained case of a strictly hereditary surname in England before the Conquest, and that they were a novelty at that time in Normandy, where the custom was taking root. After the Conquest there were instances of hereditary names in England, among the Norman families especially, if not confined to them. With these few exceptions hereditary surnames did not come into use here till about the middle of the fourteenth century.

[2] It has always seemed to the author that the prefix of "del" to the family name is more correct etymologically than "de la."

(1189). A little later, in the 3rd of John (1201), the following entry occurs in the " Rotuli de Oblatis ":

" York { The King to all, etc. Know ye that Hugh de Stueton to whom at first we wrote for his daughter for Richard de la Felda and afterwards for Robert de Carduel, has offered us 100 marks of silver that his daughter may freely marry whom she pleases and also offers to give us more if we are not contented with this, and therefore we command you if the same Robert would give us only so much as we can have from others, we will that he may have that marriage and that you cause him to have the aforesaid daughter of the same Hugh without delay."

This extract affords a curious picture of the manner in which the hands of high-born ladies were disposed of by the sovereign at that time.

In 1220 a Robert Feld was bailiff of the city of Exeter. During the next hundred years the name— somewhat varied in the spelling—occurs more and more frequently, and is found in the counties of Hereford, Lancaster, York, Hertford, Kent, Gloucester, Somerset, Oxford, and Surrey; but, for the reason already given, in all probability the persons named in these different localities bore no relationship to each other, except when residing in the same neighbourhood.

About the middle of the thirteenth century we first meet with persons of the name, who may be considered on fair and reasonable grounds to have belonged to the family to which this book relates. They are mentioned in the Coucher Book, or Chartulary of Whalley Abbey, concerning Spotland. It appears from an entry[1] in this

[1] See Appendix.

register that Adam, son of Henry del Feld, sold his house
and land at Falenge in Spotland, and that Robert del
Feld, son of the former, executed a quit claim. There
is no date to these documents; but from surrounding
circumstances they may be assigned to the middle of the
thirteenth century, or shortly after. Spotland is a suburb
of Rochdale, from which town a high road runs to
Halifax, passing by Sowerby.[1] This last-named place is
only some ten miles from Rochdale, and we find that the
Fields were seated there as early as 1306, and probably
before that date. We may fairly suppose that those of
the name residing at these two places were related, inasmuch as they were living at about the same date in the
same neighbourhood. Not improbably Adam del Feld
removed to Sowerby after selling his estate at Falenge.
This is more probable, inasmuch as we find one of the
family at Sowerby in 1333 with the uncommon name
of Adam, and as he had a house and land there in 1336,
and was dead in 1350, he was probably born as early as
1300. This Adam is described in the manor rolls as
"son of Richard del Feld," while another Adam is
mentioned as at Sowerby in 1349, who is called in them
"son of Thomas del Feld."

Although the author does not attach much importance
to the statements of Sir Bernard Burke, already referred
to, he would remark that Rochdale is in Lancashire, in
which county this writer says that Hubertus de la Feld
held lands in 1069, and that others of the name had
similar possessions there in the twelfth and thirteenth
centuries.

Before leaving this remote period, the author would

[1] Pronounced Sorby.

call attention to a branch then seated in Herefordshire, who, judging from the similarity of the arms borne respectively by them, were related to the Sowerby family.

Among the officers in the army of Charles I. was a certain Richard Symonds, a man of good family, and possessing antiquarian tastes. In the course of his wanderings with the army, he availed himself of every opportunity of visiting such objects of interest in that way as might happen to be in the neighbourhood where he was stationed. He recorded his observations in a diary written in the years 1644 and 1645, which has been published by the Camden Society. Among other ancient edifices, he visited Madley Church, about five miles from Hereford, and he describes, as follows, some ancient monuments which he saw there:

" Madley Church, com. Hereford. North window church. Kneeling figure of a knight in complete armor of the XIII century, with hands upraised in the attitude of prayer ; his sword suspended from a highly enriched belt, and his surcoat embroidered with Sable, three garbs, argent (Feld or Field), under written Walt'us et Joh'es Felde, sword between his legs;" also, " Outline of an effigy of a knight, upon which is written, ' broken, the same garbes.' Some of this family of Delafield built part of this faire churche, and a house is so called now."

The vicar of Madley wrote to the author that nothing remains of these monuments, and that the oldest existing ones in the church only date from the reign of Elizabeth. The name, however, survives in a house called " Fielde Place " and a mill adjoining styled " Fielde miil," pleasantly situated on the Wye, about a mile from the church, and in the parish. He adds that the house has been modernized, and exceeds the requirements of a farmer, though now occupied by one.

In 1558 the same coat which was on the monuments in Madley church, "differenced" by a chevron, was confirmed to John Field of Ardsley. This place is but a few miles from Sowerby, and both are in the manor of Wakefield. It will be seen hereafter that these arms were used by other members of the family residing in this manor, and at an early date.

The village of Sowerby stands on the hillside, about a mile from the river Calder, which winds through the valley beneath. The view from it is picturesque, although somewhat disfigured now by the tall chimneys of factories, which have sprung up by the riverside in the course of the last century. Behind it the land rises and attains the height of 1,553 feet at Blackstone Edge, on the Lancashire border, by which the high road passes to Rochdale. Defoe describes in his "Tour through Great Britain," a journey he made from this last place to Halifax in the month of August, 1714, when the "mountains were covered with snow," and so great were the difficulties he encountered that it took nearly the whole day to ride the eight miles from Blackstone Edge to Halifax. At the present time there are few bleaker or more dreary spots in England than the summit of Blackstone Edge.

Sowerby is a graveship in the manor of Wakefield and parish of Halifax, where the parent church stands. All baptisms, marriages, and burials of the inhabitants of Sowerby took place at this edifice, and were recorded there until 1643, when they were allowed to celebrate them in their own chapel.

HALIFAX CHURCH.

The registers of Halifax exist from 1538, the year when a decree of Henry VIII. ordered them to be kept throughout the kingdom.

Sowerby chapel, which may have contained some memorials of the Fields, was entirely destroyed by fire about the middle of the eighteenth century, and rebuilt in 1763.

The extensive manor of Wakefield belonged to the Crown from the time of the Conquest to nearly the end of the eleventh century, when William II. bestowed it on his nephew, the second Earl de Warren, whose mother, Gundreda, was daughter of the Conqueror.

It remained in the powerful family of the De Warrens for six generations, and until their extinction in 1347, when it reverted to the Crown, and continued to be a royal manor till the time of Charles I., in whose reign it was sold.

It appears, therefore, that it belonged to the sovereign during the greater part of the period when the Fields resided there.

The author has dwelt thus much on Sowerby because it may be considered in a measure the cradle of the race to which this book refers.

The existing rolls of Wakefield manor commence in 1284, but are very imperfect until 1306. A roll endorsed 1272, and called 1st roll, is a mistake for 1st of Edward II., and, therefore, 1307.

The first entry in them relating to the Fields is in 1306, and refers to a suit of Richard del Feld,[1] of

---

[1] Throughout the part of the Wakefield rolls referred to in this book the name is written "ffeld." The author has not followed this mode, as the two small letters then stood for the capital one which we now use,

Sowerby, against Robert, son of William de Saltonstall. In 1307 Thomas del Feld of Sowerby served as a juror, and in the following year Richard del Feld held a similar position, being described in the entry as "son of Roger del Feld." Very probably Richard and Thomas were brothers.

Thomas is again mentioned in 1314 and 1322, and Richard in 1314.

In 1326 John, "son of Thomas del Feld," had a dispute about land, and he is again referred to in 1334 and 1336.

In 1333 the name of Adam del Feld appears in the rolls, and in 1336 he is spoken of as holding a house and twelve acres in Sowerby, when he is called " son of Richard del Feld." This Adam is mentioned in them several times in the next fourteen years, and in 1349 he was elected greave [1] of Sowerby. He died shortly after, for an entry in 1350 states that Thomas del Feld paid heriot [2] on a house and twelve acres in Sowerby "after the death of Adam his father."

About the same time there was another Adam del Feld at Sowerby, who is named in the rolls in 1349, and called then " son of Thomas del Feld." Whether he is the Adam mentioned in them in 1393 the author is unable to say. There were also two Thomas del Felds at Sowerby who were contemporaneous, and often distinguished in the rolls as " senior " and "junior," but

and which is a modification and simplification of the double letter. A few families, like the "ffaringtons," adhere to the old style.

[1] Greave, the chief officer of a graveship.

[2] Heriot, a fine or tax paid to the lord of a manor by a person when inheriting property in it.

not always so. Thomas del Feld, junior, had a dispute in 1357 with Richard del Leighrod, which was settled by the latter paying a penalty. The former is styled in this entry " son of Adam del Feld." Later on, in 1370, "Isabella, daughter of Richard de Leghrode, deceased," was ceded by "Thomas del Feld, junior," a piece of land in Sowerby, called Todehoile. These two entries serve to show that the son of Adam del Feld was the one styled "junior."

In 1361 Thomas del Feld, junior, gave into the hands of the lord a house and sixteen acres of land in Sowerby, and "Thomas and Matilda his wife" took back the same, paying ingress.

In 1369 Thomas del Feld, junior, surrendered, and John, son of William Milner, took the half of a house and land described as "the Langeroide in Sourby in Westfelde." In the following year the same Thomas ceded a piece of land in Ribburnedene (Ripponden), to Henry Pigle. He is probably the "Thomas Feld," who, together with his wife, is assessed in the Lay Subsidy roll for the West Riding of Yorkshire, under the head of "Sourby," in the 2nd of Richard III. (1378-9).

Thomas del Feld, senior, was elected in 1364 to supervise "the agistment and pannage." In 1365 he was chosen constable, and greave in 1370. In this last year he took a piece of land of Thomas Wade in "Dedewyferode." In 1380 he hired Sowerby mill together with Thomas de Helilee, and in 1384 he served as special juror.

The name of Thomas del Feld occurs frequently in the Wakefield rolls between 1348 and 1391, without

ROGER DEL FELD
? born about 1240.

RICHARD DEL FELD
of Sowerby. Sued Rob⁴ de Saltonstall in 1306. A juror in 1308, and called then "son of Roger del Feld." Again referred to in the Wakefield manor rolls in 1314.

THOMAS DEL FELD
of Sowerby. A juror in 1307. Named in the Wakefield rolls in 1314, and also in 1322, when he was at "Halifax court."

ADAM DEL FELD
Named in the rolls in 1333. Had a house and 12 acres in Sowerby in 1336, and then styled "son of Richard del Feld." A juror in 1337, and greave of Sowerby in 1349. Dead in 1350.

JOHN DEL FELD
Named in the rolls in 1326, 1334, and 1336, when he had land at Sowerby. Called "son of Thomas del Feld."

ADAM DEL FELD
of Sowerby. Named in the rolls in 1349, and then called "son of Thomas del Feld"? also in 1393.

THOMAS DEL FELD, JUNIOR=MATILDA
Paid heriot in 1350 on a house and 12 acres at Sowerby "after the death of Adam his father." Had a dispute in 1357 with Rich⁴ del Leighrod. In 1361 surrendered to the lord a house and 16 acres at Sowerby, and took back the same, with "Matilda his wife." In 1370, Isabella, dau. of Rich⁴ de Leghrode, dec⁴, took land from him. Referred to in the rolls in 1384 and ? 1391.

In 1361 described in the rolls as the wife of Tho' del Feld.

THOMAS DEL FELD, SENIOR. Constable of Sowerby in 1365, and greave there in 1370. Hired Sowerby Mill in 1380. A special juror in 1384.

JOHN DEL FELD
Probably the eldest son. Had possession of the house and 16 acres at Sowerby which belonged to Tho' del Feld in 1361. Dead in 1393, probably without issue.

RICHARD DEL FELD
Named in the rolls in 1364. Paid heriot in 1393 on the house and 16 acres at Sowerby "after the death of John, his brother." Greave of Sowerby in 1423 and 1428. Named frequently in the manor rolls between 1393 and 1454. Probably died about last date.

AGNES DEL FELD.
ALICE DEL FELD.
Paid heriot on 15 acres and ½ of a house in "Sowerby after the death of Agnes her sister" in 1397.

See Pedigree No. 2.

the addition of "senior" or "junior," so that it is impossible to say which one is referred to in these entries. Both "senior" and "junior" are mentioned in 1384, after which date there is but one entry, in 1391, where the name is simply "Thomas del Feld." Probably both "senior" and "junior" died about this time. Others of the family mentioned in the lifetime of the two Thomas's whom I cannot place with certainty, are Elenor del Feld in 1329 and 1333, and Margaret, who paid heriot in 1357 on a cottage and land at Sowerby "after the death of John Tomson, her uncle." She is called "daughter of Thomas del Feld," but the author is unable to say of which Thomas.

In 1393 Richard del Feld paid heriot on a house and 16 acres of land in Sowerby, " after the death of John his brother," who probably left no issue. This is the same property which was in the possession of Thomas del Feld, junior, in 1361, and no doubt John and Richard were sons of Thomas and Matilda.

Richard del Feld is referred to in the rolls no less than twenty-three times between 1393 and 1454 inclusive. He must have lived to a good old age, and in all probability died about the last date.

It was during this Richard's lifetime that the prefix "del" was dropped from the family name, the wars with France having made such adjuncts unpopular. The simple name of "Feld" appears in 1412 in the rolls for the first time. After that date it is sometimes preceded by "del" and occasionally by "de," until 1446, which is the latest time at which we meet with either of these in the records referred to.

In 1427 and 1428 the name of Robert Feld occurs in

the rolls, and in the entry of the latter year he is called "son of Richard." Very possibly he was the same Robert Feld, who was elected constable of Warley in 1433, as this place is only one or two miles from Sowerby. He had a son Richard, to whom his grandfather of the same name gave in 1454 the remainder to a house and 23 acres "between Feldhouseloyne [1] on the highway of Ribbornedeyne on the south," which was then conveyed to the use of his uncle William for twenty-four years.

Richard Feld had three other sons, as appears by an entry in 1440, when he surrendered the house and land just referred to, which is described as being "between Dedewyfeclogh and Feldhouslone in Sowrby," to the use of John, son of the said Richard, with remainder to Thomas and William, brothers of John. This last immediately re-conveyed the estate to his father Richard for life. Richard Feld was chosen greave of Sowerby in 1423 and 1428. Probably the deed of 1454 was executed by him in anticipation of his immediate death.

Thomas Feld, son of Richard, who is named in the conveyance of 1440, is not again mentioned in the rolls. The author supposes that he left the neighbourhood, or died young.

William Feld, another son of Richard, was greave of Sowerby in 1476. Under date of 1508 there is an entry of the surrender of a house and 16 acres, "formerly in tenure of William Felde de Soreby," "to the use of Mabill, widow of the said William Felde, remainder to

---

[1] Loyne, Yorkshire for lane.

Hugh, son of the late John Felde, remainder to George, brother of said John." This is the same estate which Thomas del Felde, junior, and his wife Matilda held in 1361.

John, the remaining son of Richard, who is the first named of the three brothers in 1440, is again mentioned in 1443, and was a juror in 1445. He held the office of Constable of Sowerby in 1449 and 1450. He was dead in 1468, as appears by an entry in that year.

In 1397 Alice del Felde paid heriot on 15 acres, and the moiety of a house thereon "in Soureby after the death of Agnes, her sister." The author supposes that this estate was owned jointly by the two sisters, and that it is the same one which was in possession of Thomas, junior, and his wife Matilda in 1361, from whom it passed to their son John, and was inherited from him in 1393 by his brother Richard, who, the author presumes, was also the brother of these two ladies. This is all the more probable, as we find by an entry in 1508, that this property had been in possession of William Felde, who was the nephew of Alice and Agnes, if the writer's suppositions be correct, and was then conveyed to the use of his widow.

Among others of the family named in the rolls whom the author cannot place in the pedigree with certainty, are Adam del Felde, named in 1393; John Felde of Normanton in 1412, 1420, and 1423; Richard Feld of Normanton, probably son of preceding, constable in 1436, and referred to in 1446, 1447, 1449, and 1450; Matthew Feld, constable of Midgley in 1422, and Katrina de Feld of Sowerby, in 1444.

Normanton is three or four miles from the town of

Wakefield, and Midgley about half that distance from Sowerby.

In 1468 "Christopher, son of John Felde," gave heriot on a house and 23 acres, " between Dedewyfeclogh and Feldehouseloyne, after the death of John his father." He immediately surrendered the same to the use of John his brother, and to Elena, Isabella, Agnes and Johne (Joan), their sisters, for twelve years.

In 1471, " Margaret de Felde at the Overfeldhouse," was fined for encroaching on the waste. The fact of there being a Field House lane in 1440, implies the existence at that time of a Field house, while this last entry shows that there were at the date of it (1471), two buildings of that name, an upper and lower Field house. The latter is referred to in 1500, when there was a conveyance of land to Christopher Field, "between Feldhousloyne, the land of Christopher Felde and Netherfeldhous." Probably one of these is the edifice referred to hereafter, which was pulled down in the early part of this century.

Christopher Felde, who paid heriot in 1468, was elected greave of Sowerby in 1487. He is named in the rolls in 1494 and 1500, and was dead in 1509, when John, described as "son of Christopher Felde, Sowerby," paid heriot for " a house and 23½ acres, between Dedewyfeclough and Feldehousloyne, after the death of Christopher his father." " Hugh, son of late John Felde," to whom was granted a remainder to the house and 16 acres in 1508, is again named in the rolls in 1521 and 1525. At the last date he let " Feldhous " to William Brig. He is not mentioned again, and the author is inclined to think that he died childless.

John Feld, who inherited a house and 23½ acres in 1509, was doubtless the eldest son of Christopher. He was constable of Sowerby in 1513 and 1514, and was dead in 1520.

He had a brother Thomas, who, in 1492, took of the waste [1] "lying near a road in Sowerby, called Feldhousloyne," when he is described as "son of Christopher Felde;" and in 1494 he again took similar land. His name does not occur after until 1527, when he surrendered a tract of land "taken from the waste by the said Thomas," and he made a like surrender in 1530. He was dead in 1534, as appears by an entry in that year, when George Boethes and others surrender a house and land "to the use of Margaret, widow of Thomas Feld."

In 1529 there was a proclamation concerning "John Feld's land, formerly Christopher Feld's;" and in the same year this John leased the "house and 23 acres in Sourby between Dedewyfeclogh and Feldhouseloyne" to Henry Ferror.

In 1531 John Felde gave half the rent from Ferror for this property to "Elizabeth his wife" for life, and the other half to "Christopher Felde, his lawful heir." This same Christopher paid heriot on land in 1534, "after the death of Elizabeth his sister," *i.e.*, sister-in-law.

John Feld must have been the son—and, in all probability, the oldest—of the person of the same name who was dead in 1520, and therefore the brother of Christopher, who paid heriot in this year "after the decease of John his father." This is evident, not only because

---

[1] At this time there was much uncultivated land in England which was called "waste."

we find the John we are referring to in possession, in 1529 and 1531, of the house and 23 acres which Richard Feld surrendered to his son John in 1440, and which descended through him to the first Christopher in 1468, and then to his son John in 1509; but also because the John we are speaking of calls Christopher "his lawful heir" in 1531, and, more than all, because the last-named styles John's wife, Elizabeth, his "sister" when he paid heriot in 1534, after her death. The presumption is that her husband was also dead then, and that they left no son.

A Jacobus (James) Feld took of the waste in 1514, and he and Christopher are named together in the rolls in 1530. In 1534 this James surrendered land to John, Edward, and Robert his sons. Probably James was a brother of John and Christopher, and this is the more likely inasmuch as an entry in 1539 says that the last-named surrendered the reversion to half the rent of the 23 acres leased to Henry Ferrer in 1529 "to the use of John, son of Jacobus (James) Feld."

As will be seen hereafter, Christopher Feld did not marry until after the date of this surrender. His brother John was probably dead at the time, and without issue, and perhaps also his supposed brother James was no longer living, in which case the latter's son John, presumably the eldest, was then the natural heir of Christopher. This John is named again in 1532 and 1534, and at the last date, when he is described as the "son of James," he cedes a portion of his rent from the 23½ acres to the use of Edward Farrowe.

His brother Edward is not mentioned in the rolls after 1534.

Robert, the third son of James Feld, is perhaps the one of that name referred to in 1561, and also in an entry under 1594, which states that Robert Wade made a gift to Halifax "free schole" (school) "from lands formerly Robert Feilde's."

Others of the name, mentioned in the rolls, whom the author has been unable to place satisfactorily, are John Felde "of Miggelay" (Midgley), 1463, Edward Feld, 1478 and 1515, and Margaret Felde, 1548, who "formerly sang in the chapel of Sourby." She may have been the person of that name who is spoken of in 1534 as "widow of Thomas Feld."

We will now return to the second Christopher Feld, grandson of the first of the name. In 1520 he paid heriot "on 4½ acres formerly taken from the waste after the decease of John, his father." This is a smaller estate than his brother John inherited, from which I infer that the latter was the elder. In 1531 the last-named John Feld gave Christopher half the rent of the house and 23 acres which had been leased in 1529 to Henry Ferror, describing his brother as "his lawful heir." In 1539 Christopher surrendered the reversion, after his death, of half the rent of this house and land "to the use of John, son of Jacobus (James) Feld," which two were, probably, at this time, as already stated, Christopher's heirs. In the same year he gave heriot on land "after the death of Elizabeth his sister" (*i.e.*, sister-in-law).

Up to the last date, the Wakefield manor rolls have been almost the exclusive source of information relating to the family. The wills recorded hitherto have been "few and far between," but at this time are becoming more frequent, and in 1538 parish registers commenced. Fortunately, those of Halifax church exist from the beginning, which can be said of very few. One of the earliest entries in the register records the marriage of "Christopher Fyld and Grace Gradeheighe" in 1540. The baptisms of their children are entered as follows:

1541. Edward, son of Christopher Fylde, of Sowerby.
1543. Johanna, dau.   „   „   „   „
1544. Alice,   „   „   „   „   „
1545. Grace,   „   „   „   „   „
1547. John, son   „   „   „   „
1548. William, son   „   „   „   „

Among the burials we find that of John, son of Christopher Fyld of Sowerby, in 1547.

In the manor rolls there is an entry in 1554 of the surrender by Christopher Feld of two parts of 4½ acres " to the use William, Alice, and Elizabeth, his children." I do not find the name of the last among my extracts of baptisms from the Halifax registers, but as the entries are sometimes illegible, it may have been overlooked. This conveyance was doubtless made by Christopher in anticipation of his death, for in the same year (1554), his eldest son, Edward Felde, paid heriot on two parts of the 4½ acres " after decease of Grace, his mother," and "after the decease of Christopher, his father.'"

This Edward may be the one whose marriage to Isabella Greenwood is recorded in the Halifax registers in 1560, notwithstanding his youth at the time, and we find the entries of the following baptisms in them shortly after, which doubtless refer to the issue of this marriage:

1560-1. Edward, son of Edward Feild of Sowerby.
1566.   Alice, dau.   „   „   Feld „   „
1568.   Susan, „   „   „   „   „   „
1571-2. Abraham, son of „   „   „   „
1574.   Rosamond, dau. of „   „   „   „
1576-7. Samuel, son of   „   Feyld „   „

An Edward Feld of Sowerby, perhaps the father of these children, had a son Michael, whose baptism may have been overlooked for the reason given in the case of Elizabeth, daughter of Christopher Feld.

In 1597 there is an entry in the rolls of the surrender by " Edward Feld de Sowerby " of land there " to Michael his son."

This Michael took of the waste " in Blackwood-more " in 1617, and in 1634 a tract of land was ceded by Abraham Macherell "to use of Michael Feild de Blackwood."

In the parish registers the burial of " the wife of Michael Feild " is entered under date of 1639. He survived apparently until 1650, when " Michael, son and heir of Michael Feild, Blackwood," gave heriot. Some further information of this branch of the family is found in the Parish Registers of Halifax. In 1600 " Michael Feelde of Sowerby and Susan Crabtree," were married. They had a son John, baptized in 1601, while the baptism of his brother Michael, second of the name, is recorded in 1607. " Abraham Fielde of Sowerby," who was baptized in 1571-2, had daughters Sarah, baptized in 1608, and Judith in 1612. He was buried in 1623, and his daughter Sarah in 1639.

William Field, the younger of the two surviving sons

of Christopher, who was baptized in 1548, married
Susan Midgley at Halifax church in 1591, as recorded
in its registers. Her baptism took place in the same
edifice in 1574, when she is called " daughter of John
Midgley of Northowram." She belonged to an old
family of this neighbourhood—the Midgleys of Midgley
—whose arms, sable, two bars gemelle or, on a chief of
the second three caltrops of the first, were painted on
the roof of Halifax church, together with those of the
principal families who attended service there. The
residents of Sowerby worshipped at their own chapel.

The baptisms of the children of William and Susan
Field are recorded in the Halifax parish registers as
follows :

1591.   William, son of William Feild of Sowerby.
1593.   Alice, daughter of ,,   ,,   ,,   ,,
1595.   Jane,   ,,   ,,   ,, Feelde of Southowram.
1598.   George, son   ,, ,,   ,, ,, Northowram.
1600-1. Susan, daughter ,, ,,   ,, ,,   ,,
1603.   Joseph, son   ,, ,,   ,, ,,   ,,
1605.   Robert, ,,   ,, ,,   ,, ,,   ,,
1609.   Isabel, daughter ,, ,,   ,, ,,   ,,

It is clear from these entries that William Field
removed from Sowerby to Southowram within a year or
two of 1593, and we find a confirmation of this in the
Wakefield rolls, which show that Grace, daughter of
Richard Barestow, surrendered in 1594 lands in Northowram to " William Feild of Southowram." This deed
is also mentioned, under the same year, in the dockets at
Wakefield.

Shortly after purchasing this property in Northowram

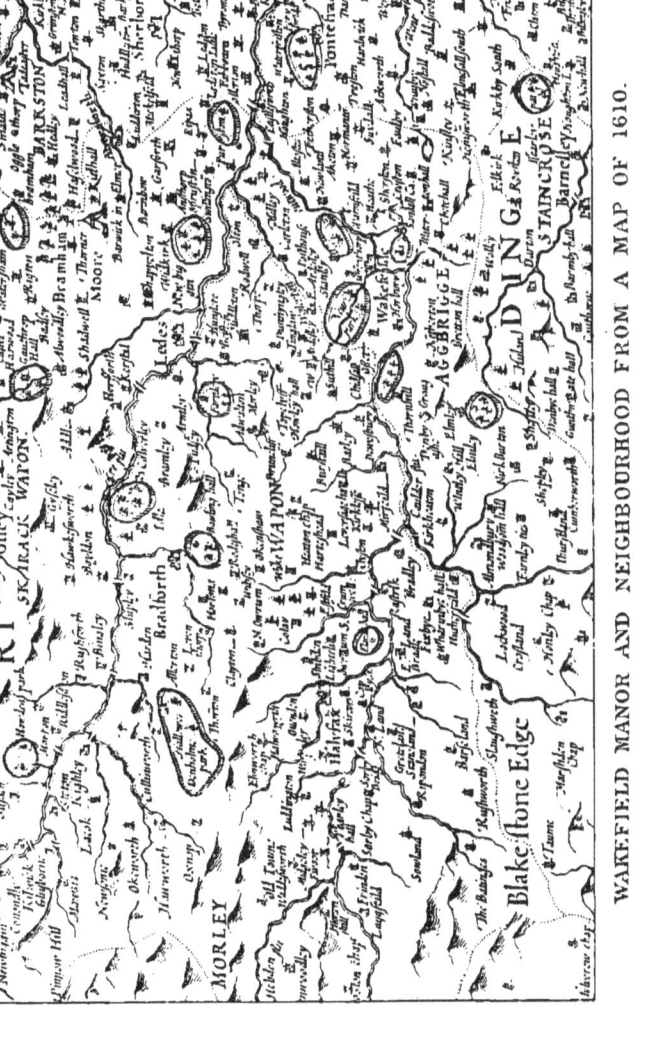

WAKEFIELD MANOR AND NEIGHBOURHOOD FROM A MAP OF 1610.

(which was the home of his wife's family), William Field removed there, where he passed the remainder of his life. There is a survey of this neighbourhood among the Duchy of Lancaster court rolls, made April 20th, 1607, in which it is stated that " William Feilde doth hold by copy of his Majesty a message called Causeye[1] and three acres of land, wherof half an acre used as pasture and an acre and a half used as arable ; " also " The same William Fielde holdeth of his Majesty, by deed from my Lord of Leicester, one acre and half a rood."

According to the Wakefield rolls, William Feild of Northowram, paid his fine in 1610 " for one tenement called Cawsey with all his coppiehold landes," and in the same year he "took of the lord 4 acres waste at Blackmyres."

In 1616 he was a juror at Brighouse court, and in 1618 he is referred to as a subtenant of William Sympson.

In this last year " William Feild Senior de le Cawsey " surrenders lands, after his decease, to " William his son and heir."

In 1619 " William Feild of Northowram, clothier, surrenders Horwithins to use of Joseph, his son." On July 15th, 1619, he made his will,[2] which is in the registry at York, and died soon after, as it was proved on the 10th November following.

In this document he calls himself " clothier," as he is

---

[1] Causeway, a road or footpath raised above the surrounding land, usually passing over a morass or damp ground. A small hamlet in Northowram is called Causeway End at the present day.
[2] See Appendix.

described also when he surrendered Horwithins in the same year.

The word "clothier" may have two meanings—a manufacturer of cloth, or a cloth merchant. William Field's calling must have been the latter. Henry VII. brought Flemish cloth weavers to England, and settled some of them at Wakefield. This industry soon became the chief one of the neighbourhood, and has continued so to the present time, when the adjacent town of Leeds is the largest cloth market in the world. At the period we are writing of, and even within the recollection of living men, all the cloth was made by hand, and in the cottages of the weavers. When a piece was finished it was taken to the merchant, or sold to him at a market where makers and buyers met. The merchant distributed the goods acquired in this way to his customers at home and abroad, and such was the high reputation of the cloths made in the neighbourhood of Wakefield, that they found their way, at this early date, to all parts of the civilized world.

Now huge mills with their machinery, driven by steam or water power, have taken the place of the hand weavers. England may be, and probably is, a richer country for the changed mode of manufacture; but is the mill hand of to-day as happy, as healthy, and, generally speaking, as well off as the workman who sat at the loom in his own cottage, breathing pure air and surrounded by his family?

Few neighbourhoods in England have suffered as much by the substitution of machinery for hand labour as this. The landscape, diversified by numerous hills and valleys, through which flowed bright and sparkling streams, was then most picturesque as well as thoroughly rural. Now tall chimneys disfigure it, darkening and poisoning the atmosphere with volumes of smoke, and the Calder is polluted by the refuse of the factories that line its banks.

Fortunately for them the old village of Sowerby and Field House stand on the hillside, and at some distance from the river, and are consequently less affected by the change than if they were nearer to it.

But we are digressing, and must return to William Field of Northowram. After providing in his will for his wife, Susan, there are legacies to his children—Jane, Joseph, Susan, Isabell, and Robert, and to Robert Rawson his son-in-law. The portions, as well as the tuition of Robert and Isabell, are committed to his brother Edward, who was, as we have shown, the only one who survived his infancy. The residue goes to his children George, Jane, Susan, Robert, and Isabell equally. His eldest son, William, was provided for by the deed of 1618, and his daughter Alice probably at the time of her marriage.

Susan, the widow of William Field, did not long survive her husband. Her will,[1] also recorded at York, is dated February 24th, 1622-3, and was proved the 14th May following. She describes herself in it as of "Black Carre."[2] This is doubtless the same place which William Field acquired in 1610, then called "Blackmyres." She gives trifling legacies to her son William and her daughter Alice, wife of Robert Rawson

---

[1] See Appendix.
[2] Carre, or Carr, an old Yorkshire word, signifying morass or swamp. "Blacker" in Northowram is mentioned as far back as 1300.

of Wrose, as they were already provided for by her late husband, and a larger one to each of her sons George and Joseph. The residue of her estate is to be divided equally between her sons Joseph and Robert, and daughters Jane, wife of John Mitchell, Susan, and Isabell. This is the last reference to Robert, the emigrant, which the author has been able to find in England.

The burials of William and Susan Field, and the marriages of two of their daughters, are entered thus in the Halifax registers:

1619. July 24th. William Feeld, of Northowram.

1623. March 6th. Widow of William Field, of Northowram.

1611. Nov. 11th. Robert Rawson, of Calverley, and Alice Feelde.

1622. June 10th. John Michell, of Thornton, and Jane Feeld.

A marriage recorded in 1638 may refer to William Field's daughter Susan, viz.:

1638. Dec. 4th. Sam¹ Holdsworth and Susan Feild, of Northowram.

William Field, the eldest son of William and Susan, remained at Northowram. It would appear from an entry in the rolls in 1627 that he married Susanna Longbothome. It reads as follows: "Thomas Longbothome de Northowram, yeoman, held lands of Earl of Leicester and Anna, wife of Lawrence Whitacres. Susanna, wife of William Feild, and Sara, wife of George Fearnley, are his 3 daughters and co-heiresses."

The births of William's children are thus recorded in the Halifax parish registers:

RICHARD DEL FELD.
(See Pedigree No. 1.)

ROBERT FELD.	JOHN FELD.	THOMAS FELD.	WILLIAM FELD.═MABILL.	GEORGE FELD.
Named in the rolls in 1428, and styled then "son of Richard Feld." ? Constable of Warley in 1433.	His father, Richard, surrendered a house and 23 acres to his use in 1449, when he is called "son of said Richard." Constable of Sowerby in 1449 and 1450. Dead in 1468.	His father, Richard, granted him in 1449 remainder to the house and 23 acres, when he is called "brother of John." who was "son of said Richard."	His father, Richard, granted him remainder to the house and 23 acres in 1449. Called then "brother of John." Greave of Sowerby in 1476. Dead in 1508. Had use of a house and 16 acres in 1508, and called then "Widow of William Felde."	In 1508 was granted remainder to the house and 16 acres, and called then "brother of the late John Feld."

RICHARD FELD.	CHRISTOPHER FELD.	HUGH FELD.	JOHN FELD.	ELENA FELD.	ISABELLA FELD.	AGNES FELD.	JOAN FELD.
In 1454 his grandfather, Richard, conveyed to him remainder to the house and 23 acres, the use of which was then given to his uncle William for 24 years.	Gave heriot in 1468 for the house and 23 acres "after the death of John his father." Greave of Sowerby in 1487. Named in the rolls in 1494 and 1500. Dead in 1509.	Was granted remainder to the house and 16 acres in 1508, when he is called "son of the late John Feld." In 1525 he let Feldhous to Wm. Brig.	In 1468, Christopher Feld surrendered the use of the house and 23 acres to "John, his brother," and the four above named females, "their sisters," for 12 years.				

JOHN FELD.	THOMAS FELD.═MARGARET.
Paid heriot on the house and 23 acres in 1509, "after the death of Christopher his father." Constable of Sowerby in 1513 and 1514. Dead in 1530.	Took of the waste in 1492, and then called "son of Christopher Felde." Named in the rolls in 1527 and 1530. Dead in 1534. The use of a house and land surrendered to her in 1534, when she is called "widow of Thomas Felde." ? Named in the rolls in 1548.

CHRISTOPHER FELD.═GRACE GLADENHIGHE.	ELIZABETH.	JAMES FELD.
Paid heriot on 4½ acres in 1520, "after the decease of John his father." In 1531 was granted by John Feld half the rent of the house and 23 acres, when he is called by the grantor "his lawful heir." Paid heriot on land in 1534 "after the death of Elizabeth his sister." In 1539 surrendered reversion to half the rent of the house and 23 acres to John, son of James Feld. Dead in 1534. Married at Halifax in 1540. Dead in 1554.	In 1529 was in possession of land "formerly Christopher Feld," and in same year leased the house and 23 acres to Henry Farrer. Probably dead and without issue in 1534. In 1531 John Feld gave half the rent of the house and 23 acres to "Elizabeth his wife" for life, and the other half to "Christopher Felde his lawful heir." Dead in 1534.	Named in the rolls in 1534. Surrendered land in 1534 to his three sons whom he names, as below.

JOHN FELD.	EDWARD FELD.	ROBERT FELD.
Named in the rolls in 1532, and in 1534 cedes part of his rent from 23 acres to Edward Farrowe. In 1539 Christopher Feld surrendered to him the reversion to half the rent of the house and 23 acres.	Named in their father's surrender of land in 1534.	

EDWARD FELD.═? ISABELLA	JOHN FELD.	WILLIAM FELD.═VIVIAN,	JOHANNA FELD.	ALICE FELD.	GRACE FELD.	ELIZABETH FELD.
bap. at Halifax, 1542. Paid heriot in 1551 "after the decease of Grace his mother," and "Christopher his father." Named in the rolls in 1597. Executor of his brother William's will 15th July, 1619.	GREENWOOD. Married at Halifax in 1560.	bap. at Halifax, 1547. Buried there same year.	bap. at Halifax, 1548. Of Sowerby till 1593. At Southowram in 1594 and 1595. Afterwards of Northowram. Bought land there in 1594, and in 1607 had a house there called Causey, and land. In 1610 acquired land at Blackmyres, and in 1619 had a place called Horwithins, both in Northowram. Will dated 16th July, 1619. Buried at Halifax 24th July following.	dau. of John Midgley of Northowram. Bap. at Halifax, 1574. Married there in 1594, and buried there 6th March, 1622-3. Will 24th Feb. same year.	bap. at Halifax, 1543.	bap. at Halifax, 1544.	bap. at Halifax, 1545.	Named in her father's deed of 1554.

See Pedigree No. 3.

See Pedigree No. 3.

1625. May 22. William, son of William Feild, of Northowram.

1627. July 8. Alice, daughter of William Feild, of Northowram.

1629. November 15. Thomas, son of William Feild, of Northowram.

1631. John, son of William Feild, of Northowram.

1634. September 14. Sarah, dau. of William Feild, of Northowram.

There is an entry in the Wakefield rolls in 1630 under Northowram that William Feild, of Cawsey, surrenders land ; and another in 1632, that " William Feild de Blackmires and Susanna, his wife," execute a quit claim to Robert Nicholls de Horton for a house in Northowram.

The following, in 1636, under the head of Hipperholme graveship, no doubt refers to him :

" William Feild died since last court."

In 1639 Susanna Feild, widow, Northowram, surrenders Leyclose to use of Matthew Sowden, and she is again mentioned in 1640 as " of Blackmyres," and in 1646 as of Northowram. Her eldest son, William Feild, born in 1625, surrenders in 1651, " 4 acres in Blackmire, Northowrom, to Jeremy Bairstowe."

Here we take leave of the Wakefield Manor rolls and the Halifax parish registers. The former were searched till 1655, and the latter till 1660. Robert Field, the youngest son of William Feild and Susan Midgley, baptized March 9th, 1605-6, emigrated to America, and will be referred to later.

Before leaving the neighbourhood of Sowerby the

E

author would say a few words of "old Field House,"
which he visited in 1878, and again in 1893. It
belongs to Colonel Stansfeld, who resides there, and in
the building adjoining called "Field House," and has
been in the possession of his family for about one hundred
and fifty years. The latter and more modern edifice
was erected in 1749 by the Stansfelds shortly after they
acquired the estate.

"Old Field House," sometimes called "the Old
Hall," judging from its architecture, dates from the
time of Elizabeth, *i.e.*, the latter half of the sixteenth
century. It is a mansion of some size, suited to the
accommodation of a numerous family, and resembling
many English manor houses of that period.

The late Colonel Stansfeld, father or uncle of the present owner, in a letter to the author, written in 1863,
said, "a much older residence of the family, on a site
about a quarter of a mile from here, was pulled down by
my father 40 years ago;" and a little later in the same year
he wrote that when this more ancient building, called
"Upper Field House," was destroyed, "in one of the
beams were found a great many gold coins of the reign
of Charles I., twenty-two of which only came into the
possession of my father, as he unfortunately happened to
be at Scarborough at the time, and it was supposed that
the workmen secured the largest portion."

The village of Sowerby is about a quarter of a mile
from "Old Field House," and a short distance beyond it
stood a third ancient building called "Fields," which
was pulled down some years since, and which doubtless
took its name from the family.

"Field Head" and "Field Bottoms" in Northowram

FIELD HOUSE, SOWERBY, NEAR HALIFAX.

are set down on the ordnance map of the neighbourhood, and these places also probably derive their appellations from the same source.

THE FIELDS OF NORMANTON AND EAST ARDSLEY.

During the fifteenth and sixteenth centuries we find branches of the family seated at several places within a short distance of Wakefield and near the neighbouring town of Bradford.

All these were doubtless offshoots of the Fields of Sowerby, although the writer cannot trace precisely their connection. None of the places referred to were more than ten or fifteen miles from that village, and most of them were nearer.

The first of the name mentioned in the Wakefield rolls at any of these localities, was John Feld of Normanton, who is referred to in 1412, and who may have been the progenitor of those of the family who were residing near a little later. This John was a juror in 1420, and he is named for the last time in 1423. Richard Feld, who was constable of Normanton in 1436, was probably his son. The wife of the latter is mentioned in the rolls in 1446, 1447, 1449, and 1450, and as she is not called " widow " in these entries, the author presumes that her husband was then living.

An examination of the parish registers of Normanton, which commence in 1538, might afford further information of this branch. It would appear from an entry in them that " Sir Thomas Feylde " [1] was the chaplain at this date.

---

[1] The title of " Sir " was often given to the clergy at this time.

An entry in the manor rolls states that Richard Felde was elected constable of " Eardeslawe " (Ardsley), in 1484. He may have been the son of Richard of Normanton.

In 1515 John Felde of " Erdeslawe " is mentioned in them. He is probably the person of the same name, who is assessed in the Lay Subsidy Roll of 6th Henry VIII. (1514-15); and again in that of 15th Henry VIII. (1523-24), under the head of " Ardeslawe," a John Feyld is named. In a similar roll of 37th of same reign (1545-46) Thomas Feelde is assessed for lands in " East-ardesley." This last is doubtless the one referred to as " Mr. Thomas Felde my brother " in the will of Richard Felde, 1542. It was made on the 19th of August in this year, and proved December 8th, 1542. He describes himself as " husbandman of the parish of Ardeslowe," and desires that " Elizabeth, my wife, and John Felde, my son, have the take of my farmhold " and makes them executors. He adds, " also I will that my children have their portion " and that " Mr. Thomas Felde my brother and Christopher Nowell be my supervisors."

The John Felde of this will was the astronomer, who has been styled " the proto-Copernican of England," inasmuch as he was the first to make known in that country by his writings the discoveries of this remarkable man, who delayed for a long time the publication of his famous work, " De Orbium Coelestium Revolutionibus," on account of the opposition and persecution to be feared from persons who considered its teachings opposed to those of the bible. Although completed in 1530, it was not printed till 1543, when its author was on his death-bed. Works based on the new system, (which revolu-

tionized the science of astronomy,) by Rheticus and
Reinhold had appeared in Germany a few years earlier,
but the " Ephemeris " of John Field for 1557, which was
published in that year, was the first opportunity afforded
to the people of England of becoming acquainted with
the true motions of the heavenly bodies. In the following year he issued a similar work, calculated for 1558,
1559, and 1560. Probably these were not his only publications, but no others have come down to us, and only
two copies of these are known to exist, the British
Museum and Bodleian Library of Oxford each possessing
both works.

John Field was probably born between 1510 and
1520. It could not have been much after the last date,
as he was co-executor of his father's will in 1542.
Wood, the historian of Oxford University, claims that
he belonged to that seat of learning, which is not
improbable, as his writings shew that he had received a
good classical education. The writer finds no mention
of him anywhere from the date of his father's will to the
publication of his first " Ephemeris," when he was
residing in London, where he may have passed the
greater part of the fourteen years intervening. A
portion of the time he, not improbably, spent abroad,
and perhaps acquired in Germany his knowledge of, and
zeal for, the new theories, which he promulgated afterwards in his native land.

By a patent dated September 4th, 1558, the heralds
formally recognized his right to the family arms : sable,
a chevron between three garbs argent, and at the same
time they granted to him the following crest :

A dexter arm issuing out of clouds fesseways proper,

habited gules, holding in the hand, also proper, a sphere
or. This appropriate crest may be considered a recognition of his services to the cause of astronomy.

We may assume that it was about 1560 that he married Jane " daughter of John Amyas of Kent," as she is
described in the Herald's visitation of Yorkshire of 1584-
85. Mr. Hunter, in an article referred to hereafter, says
that he had searched in vain the genealogical collections
of Kent without discovering anything of this lady, or her
family. This failure is easily explained by the fact that
the Amyas's were not a Kentish, but a Yorkshire family,
which had been seated in the immediate neighbourhood
of Ardsley from an early date. In all probability John
Amyas removed from here to Kent, and possibly his wife's
family belonged to that county. As far back as the 1st
of Edward I. the tolls of Wakefield Manor were let
to John de Amyas for £100 a year. His daughter
Matilda married John Waterton of Walton, whose
family has been for many centuries one of the most distinguished of this neighbourhood. The Amyas's were
seated for generations at Sandal, Horbury, and Thornhill, all of which are within half a dozen miles of East
Ardsley where John Field resided. Without having
made any special searches, the author has met with the
following references to members of this family, which
are sufficient to shew that, in all probability, John Field
chose a wife among his friends and neighbours. On
October 29th, 1481, the rector of Methley had licence
to marry " John Amias of Thornhill " and Margaret
Medley. Robert Amyas was instituted vicar of Peniston
24th May, 1498. Hunter, the historian of " South
Yorkshire," says that " he was of the Sandal family."

There are two shields carved at the end of stalls in Sandal church,—one with the Percy arms impaling first and fourth Frost and second and third Amyas,—the last coat being, on a bend three roses. The other has also the Percy arms impaling Frost, impaling Amyas. Above is the inscription " Orate pro bono statu Joselyng Pyrcy Armegery."

Jocelyn Percy was fourth son of the fourth Earl of Northumberland, and married Margaret, only child of William Frost of Beverley and Featherston. This lady inherited from her father lands in Sandal and elsewhere. Jocelyn Percy died in 1532 and his father-in-law, Frost, in 1529. We learn by the inquisition post mortem on this Jocelyn, held at Wakefield the year of his death, that Frost's wife was Ann Ranson. She was probably the second one, and the first, and mother of Margaret, an Amyas. The parish registers of Roystone, which is some five miles south of Sandal, begin in 1558. There are several entries in the earlier part, which relate to persons of the name of Amyas, as, for instance, the burial of Elizabeth Amyas in 1569 and the baptism of " Beatris " Amyas in 1585.—The author fancies that John Field returned to East Ardsley not long after his marriage. We find him there at the time of the Herald's Visitation of Yorkshire in 1584-85, when he recorded the names of his wife and children, but for some reason, which the writer cannot explain, did not give the names of his ancestors, nor even that of his father.

As stated already, his wife's name is entered at this visitation as " Jane the daughter of John Amyas of Kent," and his children are given as follows : " Richard Feld, eldest son, aged twenty-two, in 1585, Matthew second son, Christopher third son, John fourth son, Thomas fifth son, William sixth son, James seventh son, Martyne eighth son," and a daughter Anne.

John Field's [1] will, recorded at York, is dated December 28th, 1586, and was proved May 3rd following. He styles himself " fermer sometymes studente in the mathy mathicale sciences," and desires to be buried [2] within the parish church porche of Ardeslowe. He disinherits his eldest son in these words : " I do give to my disalyall and loose lyved sonne Richard Feild one sylver spoone in full payment and satisfacon of his child's porcōn wth wch yf he be not satisfied I will he lose the benefyt of the same." He names in it, his wife Jane, whom he appoints executrix, and there are legacies " to James Feild and Martyne Feild, my two youngest sonnes," and to several friends and servants. The residue is to be divided among his eight children. Jane Field survived her husband till 1609. Her will, which is dated July 17th of that year, names Marie, daughter of Richard Feild, her son, Matthew and his children, and her sons William, Thomas, James and Martin.

Christopher and John were no doubt dead, as they are not mentioned in their mother's will, and as she calls Thomas her third son.

Matthew Field, second son and heir of the Astronomer, remained at Ardsley. In the Wakefield Manor rolls there is an entry in 1596, of an indenture by which William Hall of Settle and Elizabeth,[3] his wife, " cosyn

---

[1] See Appendix.

[2] Only persons of consequence were buried in the church.

[3] She is called in this entry " Elizabeth Nowell," and as her maiden name was certainly Field, the writer presumes that Hall was her second

and heire of Matthewe Feilde of London, deceased"
surrender a house in Wakefield and lands in Wrenthorpe to Matthew Feilde of Ardislowe, gentleman"
and Matthew Watkinson of same place. This document
serves to shew a relationship between the branch of the
family seated at Ardsley and that residing at Sandal or
Crofton, which will be referred to hereafter.

In 1601 William Walkhead of Woodhouse bequeaths
to "Mr. Matthew Field of Ardsley an old angel[1] to
make him a ring." His name occurs in the wills of
three inhabitants of Ardsley dated respectively 1607,
1608 and 1609. He bought the manor of Thurnscoe
from the coheirs of Sir John Constable in, or prior to
1614, and about the same time—conjointly with his
brother William—the fourth part of the manor of Idle
of Sir John Savile. On July 6th, 1617, together with
"James Field, gentleman," his son and heir apparent,
he gave a bond to Richard Waterhouse, of Clayton in
Bradford, for the fulfilment of certain covenants. He
was one of the collectors of the subsidy for the West
Riding of Yorkshire in 1623.

The marriages and burials in the parish registers of
East Ardsley do not commence till 1654 and the baptisms
till 1662 ; but tolerably perfect copies of the entries for
some of the earlier years exist in the Archbishop's registry
at York, from which I make the following extracts :

husband. Christopher Nowell was a supervisor of the will of Richard
Field in 1542, and John Field in his will in 1586 makes a bequest to "my
cousine Nowell."

[1] Angel, a gold coin, so called because it bore an image of St. Michael
and the dragon.

BAPTIZED.

1602 April 3, Matthew son of Matthew Feild, Gent.
1604 March 25 Judith dau.   ,,   ,,   ,,
1608-9 Mar. 12 Matthew son   ,,   ,,   ,,
1610-11 Jan. 27 John   ,,   ,,   ,,   ,,

MARRIED.

1627 Oct. 27 William Forman and Anne Feild.

BURIED.

1602 Dec. 30, Matthew son of Matthew Feild, Gent.
1609 Aug. 30 Jane Field
1632 June 14 Margaret wife of Matthew Feild.

Matthew Feilde, the astronomer's son, had other
children than those named, as appears by the will of his
son Matthew referred to later.

The elder Matthew died June 2nd, 1631, and on
September 9th following, an inquisition post mortem
was held at Doncaster relative to his estate at Thurnscoe,
from which it appears that he died possessed of the
manor of that name and of a mansion called Thurnscoe
Grange; also, that on April 5th, 1631, Henry Shaw,
Gervase Smith, and William Forman, who had married
the daughters of the aforesaid Matthew, relinquished all
right they might have to the manor of Thurnscoe to
James Feild, eldest son and heir of Matthew Feild, then
aged forty years.

This James, who was born in or about 1591, resided
at Thurnscoe, and the parish registers of that place
contain the following entries relating to him :

BAPTIZED.

1628 Aug. 17. James Feild son of James Feild and
Margaret his wife.

1632 Jany. 27. Robert Feild, son of James Feild and
Margaret his wife.

1639 Jany. 23. Anne Feild dau. of James Feild and
Margaret his wife.

BURIED.

1640 April 9. Anne Feild dau. of James Feild and
Margaret his wife.

Some of the entries for 1630 are quite obliterated,
but the copies at the registry at York supply the loss,
and shew that William, son of James Field and Margaret
his wife, was baptized on May 4th in that year.

Matthew Field, grandson of the astronomer, and
eldest surviving brother of James, resided and died at
East Ardsley. His will was dated January 10th, 1638-9,
and was proved the 19th of April following. He values
his estate at "noe less than fourteen hundred pounds."
He leaves £400 to his son Matthew, who appears to have
been his only child, and gives him the disposal of £100,
when he is sixteen years of age. There is a legacy of
£20 to his brother James, and " to his daughter Judith
Feild, now with me, Fyve pounds." To brother William
Feild £20. To brother John Feild £30. To " my
cozen (nephew) Gervis Smith, who is at Cambridge,
five pounds." To " my syster Shawe forty shillings."
To " my syster Anne Forman twenty pounds." To my
brother Gervais Smith's children, equally, £10. He

speaks of his brother James' children. There are other legacies to friends, servants, and the poor of Ardsley. He appoints " my father-in-law Mr. Robert Feild, my brother James Feild and my brother-in-law Gervis Smith supervisors." The entry in the East Ardsley registers shews that his wife, Margaret, died before him. William Feild, sixth son of the astronomer, resided at Thurnscoe, and married Jane, daughter of John Sotwell, vicar of Peniston, and widow of George Burdett of Carhead, parish of Silkstone, where she was buried October 21st, 1623. The author has no evidence of their having issue. He is unable to give any information of the remaining sons of the astronomer, and supposes that his only daughter, Anne, died young.

Before leaving this branch of the family, the author would like to say a few words about a pamphlet, which was published some years since in America, and according to which Robert Field of Flushing, the emigrant, was born in 1610, and was son of James, grandson of Matthew, and great grandson of John Field, the astronomer, and that Zechariah Field, who was in New England about 1632, was son of John, and grandson of the astronomer.

Much as the author would wish to have so distinguished a man as ancestor, truth compels him to say that there is no foundation for these statements. As regards the ancestry of Robert Field, he thinks it is sufficiently proved in this book, and there is every reason to suppose that John Field, the fourth son of the astronomer, was dead and without issue at the date of his mother's will in 1609, as neither he, nor any child of his, is referred to in it; although there are legacies to

Mary, daughter of her son Richard, and to her son Matthew's children. The author would refer those who are interested in this question [1] to an article in the "New England Historical and Genealogical Register" for April, 1868.

Although John Field was one of the most distinguished pioneers in the cause of science of whom England can boast, his memory has been almost entirely and unjustly neglected by his countrymen, and, even in astronomical circles, his name is hardly, or not at all, known.

Those who are desirous of learning something more of this distinguished man, will find all that the writers have been able to glean of him, in an article by the Rev. Joseph Hunter, in the " Gentleman's Magazine " for May, 1834, and in a supplementary one by the author, in the number for November, 1862. He would observe that he now thinks the suggested ancestry of Richard, father of John Field, in his article, erroneous, and that the fact of there being two Matthews—one a son and the other a grandson of the astronomer—led to some confusion, and they are wrongfully treated as the same individual in it.

[1] The author has met with the name of Zachariah Field but three times in the course of his searches in England : Francis Field, of Middleton Stoney, co. Oxford, names brother Zachary Feild, deceased, in his will dated 1616. Ellen Feild, of Chipperfield, parish of King's Langley, co. Herts, in her will in 1652, names her son Zachary Feild; and William Feild, of St. Paul's, Covent Garden, London, speaks of son Zacharias in his will in 1674. None of these could have been Zechariah, the emigrant.

THE FIELDS OF CROFTON, SANDAL, AND WAKEFIELD.

The villages of Crofton and Sandal adjoin. They
are both in the manor of Wakefield, and some two or
three miles from the town of that name. About the
same distance north-east of Crofton is Normanton, where
John Feld was residing from 1412 to 1423. Between
these two places lies the parish of Warmfield, in which
another John Feld was living in 1514-15 at a place
called Sharlston, in Warmfield. A very few years later,
we find persons of the name at Crofton and Sandal,
which looks as if the descendants of John of Normanton
had spread themselves to these two villages through the
intervening parish of Warmfield. In the Wakefield
Manor rolls, under the head of Sandal, there is a reference
in 1520 to lands formerly in the tenure of Robert Felde
and Agnes, his wife; and in the subsidy roll of the 15th
Henry VIII. (1523-4) " Robert Feylde " and " William
Feylde " are assessed under the head of Crofton.

Before proceeding further, the author would say that
at Sandal stood the famous castle of that name, which
was the chief seat of the manor from an early period,
and often the abode of royalty. During the civil wars
it was besieged and captured by the Parliamentary forces
in 1645, and destroyed shortly after, so that only its
ruins remain. At the period of which the author is
writing, Sandal was a more important place than
Crofton, and it is not improbable that residents of the
latter and neighbourhood should be sometimes described
as "of Sandal." It is, therefore, not unlikely that the
Robert of the manor rolls and he of the subsidy roll was

the same individual. As we get on, a difficulty arises in tracing the relationship of the different members of this branch of the family, from the frequent occurrence of this name and that of Christopher, and the author would remark here, that both of these were very common about this time among the Fields of Sowerby.

On the 27th February, 1529-30, "William Feld of Crofton," (whom the author takes to be the person assessed in 1523-4,) made his will, in which he speaks of his wife, his daughter Margaret, and his son Christopher; whom he appoints executor. It is uncertain if the Robert Field, who made his will in 1558, is the one assessed at the same time as William, or not. He describes himself as of Crofton. There are bequests in it to my brother Christopher and the daughter of the latter, also to his brother Charles, and to Robert and Alice Feild, and their children, Robert and Alice. As the testator had a brother Christopher, he may have been a son of William, although, in that case, not named in his father's will of 1529-30.

Two Christopher Fields witnessed the will of " Christopher Rishworthe of Crofton, gentleman," in 1538— one describing himself as " husbandman " and the other as " wardroper." The wills of these two witnesses— referred to later—can be identified. The writer supposes that all the following entries in the manor rolls refer to Christopher the " wardroper."

In 1541 he surrendered lands in Wakefield graveship and manor to Elizabeth his wife.

In 1544 he is spoken of as " Christopher Feld of Sandall, merchant," and in 1547, under the head of this place, it is stated that he was elected greave for

lands formerly Thomas Shey's. This entry occurs in
1552 : " Robert Copley redd. lands to Christopher Feld,
Sandall." His will is dated July 8th, 1557, and was
proved December 18th of the same year. He describes
himself as " Christopher Feylde of Wakefield,[1] mercer,"
and desires to be buried in the church of Wakefield,
near his wife. He directs his executors " to cause a
troughe stone with a remembrance of himself wife and
children in pictures of brass to be set upon and laid upon
the grave " as soon after his burial as convenient. There
are legacies to his brother Nicholas Feild, if he is living,
to his son Christopher Feild and to Percival Feild, to
daughter Elizabeth, wife of Henry Watkinson, to
daughter Katharine, wife of Richard Atkinson, to Anne
Browne, daughter of said Katharine, to every one of the
children of the said Elizabeth Watkinson, to Roger and
Nicholas Jowett, his sister's children, to his son Matthew's
wife and others. The residue is left to Matthew
Feild, his son and heir, whom he appoints executor
together with testator's brother William and others.
The Rev. J. L. Sisson, in his " Historical Sketch of
Wakefield Church," published in 1824, speaks of the
monuments formerly in this edifice, and gives the following inscription on that of Christopher Field, which stood
in the north aisle : " Here under this stone lyeth buried
the bodies of Christopher Fylde mercer and Eliz. his
wyfe which Christopher deceased the 30th day of
November in the year of our Lord God[2] 1558. On
whose soul Jesus have mercy."

---

[1] Probably his place of business was at Wakefield, and his residence at
Sandal, or Crofton.
[2] The author cannot explain the slight discrepancy in the dates of this

Christopher, the husbandman, made his will, December 1st, 1570, describing himself in it as "Christopher Feild of Crofton." There are legacies in it to his son Robert Feild, and to his, Robert's, wife and children Christopher, Frances, Elizabeth, and Alice, also to Isabel and Frances, children of his son John, to whom he leaves the residue and appoints executor. He bequeaths to each of three of the children of his son Robert "one ewe lamb," which makes it pretty evident that his calling was that of "husbandman." His will was proved March 13th, 1570-71.

Probably one of the two Christophers was the son of William Field, who made his will in 1529-30; but if so, the author is unable to say which.

Matthew, son and heir of Christopher Field, mercer, removed to London, and apparently carried on the same business there that his father had done at Wakefield. We learn from a pedigree of the Meredith family among the Harleian MSS. at the British Museum, that he married Elizabeth, daughter of Robert Meredith of London, Mercer, and his wife Jane, daughter of Sir William Loke, Knt., and that this Elizabeth was co-heiress of her brother William, who died childless. Matthew Field resided at Hackney in a mansion called " the Black and White House," supposed to have been built by him, and he was a member of the " Mercers' Company," one of the most ancient and wealthy of the London guilds. We learn by the Wakefield Manor rolls that he was elected in 1569 " greave for Shay's land, deputy William Sykes."

monument and of the will. It may arise from an error in copying from the registry at York the year when the will was proved, or be a mistake of the person who wrote the inscription.

His father, Christopher, was elected to this same office in
1547, as already stated.   The manor of Kingshold forms
part of the present suburb of London, called Hackney,
and in its rolls we find several references to Matthew
Field. In 1568, Wm. Alman and Elizabeth his wife (formerly wife of Wm. White, deceased), made a surrender
to " Matthew Feylde, Citizen and Mercer of London."
In 1570, Henry White, son of the above William, in
1575 Joshua White, one of the heirs of Wm. White,
and Elizabeth his wife, and in 1576 Thomas White, one
of the sons of the aforesaid Wm. White, of Hackney,
and Eliz. his wife, all made similar surrenders to
Matthew Feild, of London, Mercer.   An entry in the
Kingshold Manor rolls of January 19th, 1581-82, says,
" A presentment is made that Matthew Feild is dead and
that Elizabeth Feild of Wakefield, co. York, is dau. of
Christopher Field, brother of the s^d Matthew."

Matthew Field seems to have died childless and left
no will.   We find an entry in the records of the Prerogative Court of Canterbury, in London, that administration was granted to Anthony Marler on the estate of
Matthew Field of St. Laurence, Old Jewry, Mercer, on
April 1st, 1581.   His burial is recorded, in the registers
of that church, on January 19th,[1] 1580 (*i.e.* 1580-81).

In the Hall of the Mercers' Company of London, of
which Matthew Field was a member, is an old oak
carving, consisting of a shield with the arms of the
guild, and underneath another, with those of Field (a
chevron between three garbs), impaling two other coats,—
one a lion rampant, the other a chevron between three

---

[1] One of the figures is indistinct in the author's copy, and it may be
the 12th of January.

dolphins, the last being the arms of Meredith. This carving was formerly in Matthew Field's residence, " the Black and White House " already referred to, and when it was pulled down some years since, William Tyssen, Esq., the then lord of the manor in which it stood, presented the carving to the Mercers' Company.

We find some notices of Elizabeth Field, niece and heiress of Matthew, in the Wakefield Manor rolls, viz. : 1580, Elizabeth Field, daughter of Christopher Field, brother of Matthew Field, dec^d paid V^s iij^d heriot· for " 3 shoppes in le m^r ketstead ^{1} de Wakefield, close of 2 acres in Alverthorpe, 4 closes (8 acres), in Wrenthorpe and Woodall in Stanley, post dec. of Matthew her uncle ": 1583, " Elizabeth Field, cousin (*i.e.* niece) and heir presumptive of Matthew Field, dec^d redd, Woodside close in Wrenthorpe (6 acres), to Thomas Cave."

It would appear from the following that Elizabeth Field married first a Nowell, and secondly, William Hall : 1596. Indenture 39th Elizabeth, " William Hall of Settle, yeoman and Eliz. Nowell his wife, cosyn (niece), and heir of Matthew Field of the Citie of London dec^d of the one part and Matthew Watkinson of Ardeslowe, chapman, and Matthew Feilde of Ardislowe, gentleman, of the other part, surrender to the two latter, house, shopp, with chambre over, in Wakefield and 8 acres in Wrenthorpe at £5 per annum rent." This entry shews that there was a connection between the branch of the family, of which I have been writing, and that of East Ardsley. The last Matthew Field referred to above was the second son and heir of John Field the

^{1} Market-place.

astronomer, whose will contains a legacy " to my cosine
Nowell and Christopher his son." This " cosine
Nowell " was perhaps the first husband of Elizabeth
Field. Matthew Watkinson may have been a son of
her aunt Elizabeth and Henry Watkinson, both of whom
are named in the will of Elizabeth Field's grandfather,
Christopher, in 1557.

Robert Field of Wakefield made his will August 29th,
1599, and mentions in it his wife Rosamond and
daughters Elizabeth, Alice, and Margaret. It will be
noticed that two of the grandchildren of Christopher
Field, whose will was made in 1570, were named
Elizabeth and Alice, which leads the author to suppose
that their father Robert—also mentioned in that will—
was the same individual as the one who made his in
1599.

A " William Feild de Wakefield " is named in the
rolls in 1611, and in the same year " Roger Feilde de
Wakefield, chapman " took of waste in Alverthorpe.
This Roger is more fully referred to under Alverthorpe.
In 1633, and again in 1634, " William Feild de Wakefield " grants lands to his wife Elizabeth, and in the
latter year, under Wakefield, Elizabeth Field surrenders
Bascynge to Thomas Bedford and Mary his wife, a
daughter of William Field; remainder to Edward, son
of said William, who was probably dead at the time.

The following is entered in the rolls in 1612:

" William Feilde, civis and Marchante tayler de
London & Sara ux. eius surrender vac. voc. Lowefeild
(Wakefield) to John Lyon of Wakefeild, gent, money
to be paid at his house in the p͡sh of St. Faith, London."
It does not follow that the calling of this William was

that of tailor, for many who had no such occupation,
joined this wealthy guild for the valuable privileges con-
ferred on its members. His will is recorded in the
Prerogative Court of Canterbury at London. It is dated
January 28th, 1621-22, and was proved February 13th
following. He styles himself " Citizen and Merchant
Taylor." He leaves to four friends in trust "all my
lands and teñts in Hawness and Chapwell, Co. Beds."
The personality to be divided between his wife, Sarah,
and his children. There are legacies as follows : To my
wife Sarah £100, out of my lands at Lambeth. To
twenty poor people of this parish of St. Faith, each 20*s*.
To my brother John Chapman 20*s*. for a ring. To
my brother Warner and my sister each 20*s*. To my
mother 20*s*. He appoints his wife, Sarah, sole executrix.
His widow survived him for more than thirty years.
Her will is dated July 30th, 1653, and was proved
November 10th, 1657. She describes herself as " Sarah
Field of St. Faith's under St. Paul's widow " " aged and
weak," and directs her debts to be paid out of her leases
in St. Paul's church yard and Old Change. There are bequests to my granddaughter Mary, wife of Oliver Boteler
of Harrold, Co. Bedford; to my son-in-law, William
Jeston and his wife, Mary; to my son-in-law, Robert
Thornton ; to Adam Howes, and to her, the testator's
daughters, Sarah Thornton and Elizabeth Howes. She
speaks of her eldest son Samuel, deceased; of her son
James, and of her grandchild William Feild. Her
burial is thus recorded in the parish registers of St.
Faith's: " 1657 May 4. Mrs. Feild out of St. John's,
chancel." [1] In the same registers are recorded the follow-

[1] Meaning that she was buried in this part of the church. The

ing baptisms of children, who were probably the issue of her grandson, William :

1656.　July 1.　William, son William Field, woolen Draper and Elizabeth, St. Paul's churchyard, born 30th June.

1656-7.　Mch. 20.　Elizabeth dau. of same, born 19th.

1657-8.　Mch 4.　Daniel, son of same, born 25 Feby

1659.　Oct 15.　Nathaniel, son of same, born 11th

1661.　July 2.　Elizabeth, dau. of same, born 28th June.

Under the head of burials are the following :

1657.　April 7.　Elizabeth dau. William Feild, Woolen Draper and Elizabeth, Pauls chch y^d.

1657.　May 4.　Mrs. Feild out of St. John's. Chancel.

1661.　July 22.　Nathaniel and Elizabeth, son and dau of William and Elizabeth Feild.

1664.　April 7.　Samuel, son of same.

Probably the parish registers of Wakefield, which begin in 1613, and those of Crofton, which date from 1617, may afford additional information of the Fields residing in these localities after the dates named. Those of Sandal do not commence till 1652.

The author would mention, before completing his account of the different members of the family, formerly living in these three parishes, that an old house on the

author supposes that the words "out of St. John's" mean that she was residing in that parish at the time of her death, but that her husband was buried in the church of St. Faith's, and, as she wished to lie beside him, was interred there.

south side of the street at Crofton has on it the arms of the Fields of Wakefield Manor, viz., a chevron, between three garbs. Doubtless this dwelling was the abode of one of the family, and was probably built by him.

THE FIELDS OF HEATON, SHIPLEY, AND BRADFORD.

About eight miles north-east of Halifax, and six miles from North Owram, is the flourishing and populous town of Bradford. A branch of the Fields was residing in its environs in the earlier part of the fifteenth century. The author has not made as thorough searches into the history of this branch, as in the case of that residing in Wakefield Manor, and further investigations may bring new facts to light concerning it. The parish registers of Bradford do not commence till 1596, and therefore afford no very early information of the family. From the time of Edward Feild of Horton, 1595, and his five brothers and same number of sisters, down to the birth of the two daughters of John Wilmer Feild, he has followed the pedigree recorded in the College of Arms, London, where proofs of its authenticity would have been required before entering it.

On the 12th of March, 1429, " Thomas del Felde de Bolton "[1] made his will, leaving to his wife Isabel all his lands and tenents " in villa and tertory de Bynglay " for life, remainder to his heirs. After the death of " Anabelle my mother," his son Robert is to have his

---

[1] Bolton, near Heaton and Shipley. In Domesday survey Chellow, in the township of Heaton, is noted as one of the dependencies of Bolton Manor.

lands " in villa and tertory of Bradford," and if Robert die without issue, remainder to William, his brother.

On the 21st of April, 1480, letters of administration on the estate of William Feld, of Bradford, were granted to his widow Katherine Feld.

Thomas Feilde, of Shipley, in his will dated January 14th, 1572-73, desires to be buried in the south side of the church of Bradford. He bequeaths to his wife Anne for life, the farmhold where he dwells, also two new mills and a farmhold occupied by Richard Lillie. After her death, these properties and a tenement to go to daughter Frances Feilde, or if she die without heirs, to brother William, to whom he leaves two tenements in Great Horton, one of which is in the occupation of Percival Feild. His father, John Feilde, is one of his executors. The author is unable with certainty to connect this Thomas with the pedigree, but thinks it is not impossible that his brother William was the father of the eleven children, of whom Edward is the first named. The "widow Feilde of Shipley," who was buried at Bradford, October 28th, 1599, was, he supposes, wife of Thomas.

William Feild, of Great Horton, made his will March 3rd, 1598-99, and names in it his wife Jennett and "younger children" Frances, Marie, Alice, and Thomas, each of whom was to receive successively the rents of his lands in Bradfordtowne until they had got their respective portions. There was an elder child, John, as shewn hereafter, and perhaps others. His burial is entered as follows in the Bradford church registers: " 1599, May 23d William Feilde of Horton." There is a later entry on June 14th, 1612, of the burial of "widow Feild of Horton in the church," which probably refers to his wife. This William may have been the brother of that name whom Thomas Feilde refers to in his will in 1572-73; although it is strange, in that case, that the former should have named but three of the eleven children at the beginning of the pedigree, when he executed a similar document in 1598-99; but it must not be overlooked that these three, Marie, Alice, and Thomas, are mentioned both at the head of the pedigree and in William's will. We find a reference to the last-named a little later. On September 2nd, 43rd Elizabeth (1601), an inquisition post mortem was held at Shipton after the death of William Feilde, of Great Horton, yeoman, who died May 23rd, 41st Elizabeth (1599). It was found that he had houses and lands in Great Horton and in Bradford, and that his son John, aged fifty years and more, was his heir.

We now come to the pedigree recorded in the Heralds' College, to which the writer has occasionally added remarks. It commences with Edward Feild, of Horton, 1595 and 1601, after of Shipley, 1615. Died April 6th, 17th Charles I. (1641), buried at Bradford 15th of same month, inquisition post mortem August 23rd following. He married Janet Thornton at Bradford, August 7th, 1599. She was buried in Bradford Church May 9th, 1643. Thomas Feild, brother of Edward, married at Bradford October 25th, 1596, Sybil Roode, or Rode. Among the baptisms at Bradford are those of the following children of Thomas Feild, of Horton; but as there is no mention of them in the pedigree, the author is not sure that Thomas and Sybil Feild were

H

their parents. Frances, baptized 1613; William, 1615; Mary, 1616-17; Thomas, 1619; John, 1620-21; and Richard, 1623. Other brothers and sisters of Edward in the pedigree are William, Anne, Elizabeth, Susan, Mary, Alice, Robert, George, and John. Robert, described as of Shipley, clothier, is named in a deed of 1595. Died November 2nd, 1599, buried at Bradford November 12th same year. Will dated November 5th, 1599, inquisition post mortem March 27th, 42nd Elizabeth. He names in his will his brothers George, Edward, John, and William; and his sisters Elizabeth, Alice, Anne, Susan, Sybil, Mary, and Isabel; also Jane, daughter of brother William, and John and Alice, children of brother Thomas.

George Feild, another brother of Edward, is set down as of Shipley, and forty-seven years old at the death of his brother Robert. He married Isabel Mortimer at Bradford, August 7th, 1599. The author finds a George, son of George Feild, of Shipley, baptized at Bradford November 28th, 1602, whom he supposes to be the issue of this marriage. No particulars are given of John Feild, the last-named brother of Edward. The pedigree indicates that all three brothers, Thomas, William, and George, left issue, although no children are named.

Joseph Feild, eldest son and heir of Edward, was baptized at Bradford August 22nd or 23rd, 1601. He remained at Shipley, and was lord of the manor of Heaton October 30th, 1635. His wife was Mary, daughter and co-heiress of William Rawson, of Braken Bank, parish of Keighley. Joseph Feild's will is dated August 25th, 1660, and was proved January 9th, 1661.

He names in it his wife Mary, sons John and Jeremy,
and daughters Mary and Anne; the latter, wife of
William Parkinson. Also his grandchildren Joseph and
Mary, children of his son Jeremy. Mary, widow of
Joseph Feild, was buried at Bradford May 5th, 1663.
The following children of Joseph and Mary are named
in the pedigree. Anne, baptized at Bradford January
18th, 1626-27, married to William Parkinson, both
living August 25th, 1660; John, eldest son and heir,
baptized March 30th, 1628, of Heaton. Will made
about October 13th, 1712. Buried at Bradford October 18th same year. Administration granted at York
June 16th, 1713. Joshua, baptized at Bradford March
27th, 1631, buried there November 14th, 1632. Jeremiah, second son, baptized at Bradford July 27th, 1634,
living at Hipperholme from 1660 to 1672, after of
Chellow in Heaton, where he died; buried May 7th,
1705. He married at Bradford November 2nd, 1658,
Judith, daughter of William Walker, of Scoles, in the
parish of Birstall. It would appear from the pedigree
that John, eldest son of Joseph and Mary Feild, was
never married.

The children of Jeremiah and Judith Feild are re-
corded as follows. Joseph Feild, eldest son and heir,
baptized at Halifax March 10th, 1660; sometime of
Chellow, after of Shipley and Heaton. Will dated
March 1st, 1728, codicil April 11th, 1729; proved
July 6th, 1733. Died without issue. Mary, baptized
at Halifax January 11th, 1662; married at Bradford,
May 1st, 1685, to Paul Greenwood. John Feild, of
Chellow in Heaton, second son, married Grace, daughter
of Timothy Rhodes, of Heaton, and relict of Thomas

Hodgson, of Little Horton, in the parish of Bradford. Buried at Bradford January 18th, 1731, and his wife Grace, December 5th, 1702. Sarah Feild, of Bradford, died unmarried May 11th, 1758, at a great age. Anne, baptized at Halifax May 8th, 1671. Abig. il, baptized at Halifax March 16th, 1672; married to George Longbotham of that town; living, a widow, March 1st, 1728.

The author omitted to state that John Feild, after the death of his first wife, Grace, married, May 27th, 1708, Susan, daughter of John Binns, of Allerton, at Bradford, where this lady was baptized April 17th, 1687. She was living, a widow, in 1749. John Feild had by this second wife, Susan, a daughter, Mercy, baptized at Bradford September 9th, 1708, who died young, buried November 30th, 1716. Jeremiah, baptized February 10th, 1709-10, buried at Bradford September 2nd, 1718; and Jonathan, baptized March 4th, 1714, buried March 21st, 1715, at Bradford. John Feild had issue by his first wife, Grace, John Feild, of Heaton, eldest son and heir, 1728; died January 18th, 1772, aged seventy-one, buried at Bradford. Administration granted at York February 22nd, 1772. He married Mary, only daughter of Joshua Eamonson, of Seacroft; marriage settlement dated 1733. She died February 5th, 1750, in her forty-first year, and was buried at Bradford. Judith Feild, daughter of John and Grace, married Henry Atkinson, of Bradford; marriage settlement dated December 29th, 1733; living 1751. John Feild and Mary Eamonson had issue.

Mary, eldest daughter, died January 11th, 1747, aged sixteen; buried at Bradford. Anne, born August 2nd,

1735, buried at Bradford July 2nd following. John
Feild, eldest son and heir apparent, baptized August
25th, 1738; died unmarried December 16th, 1758;
buried at Bradford. Anne, born January 18th, 1739,
died unmarried at Bristol May 31st, 1760, and buried
in St. Augustine's Church there. Sarah, baptized November 20th, 1741, died unmarried October 29th,
1758; buried at Bradford. Joshua Feild, of Heaton,
youngest son, baptized at Bradford December 31st, 1742,
died September 25th, 1819; buried at Bradford. He
married Mary, younger daughter and surviving heir of
her father, Randal Wilmer; baptized at St. Cuthbert's,
York, September 17th, 1751; marriage settlement dated
September 7th and 8th, 1774; married at Scarborough
October 4th, 1774; living 1821.

The children of Joshua Feild and Mary Wilmer were
John Wilmer Feild of Heaton, Esq., eldest son and heir,
Lord of Heaton, Shipley, Barnby-moor and Allerthorpe
cum Waplington. Born August 20th, 1775. Baptized
at the Church of the Holy Trinity in York. Died
1839. He married Anne, eldest daughter of Robert
Wharton Myddleton, Esq., of Grimble Park, in Cleve-
land, Co. York, at Easington, September 3rd, 1812.
She died February 11th, 1815, and was buried at
Crambe, near Melton, Co. York. His second wife was
Isabella Helena, daughter of Captain Salter, R.N., whom
he married in 1839. This lady is not named in the
pedigree, as it was recorded before her marriage. Zachary
Feild, another son of Joshua and Mary, was born January
7th, 1777. Died an infant. Joshua Feild, of Leeds,
second surviving son of the same couple, born May 10th,
1778, and baptized the 13th of same at York. Lord of

Berrythorp and Kennethorpe. He married Elizabeth, eldest daughter of William Wainman, of Carrhead, in Craven, Co. York, Esq., at Kilnurch, August 17th, 1801. Mary Anne, eldest daughter of Joshua and Mary, was baptized May 8th, 1779, married at Goodram Gate, February 4th, 1802, to Eugene Thomas Whittell, sometime of Over Helmsley. He died about June 20th, 1821, and was buried at Chelmsford. Delia, her younger sister, born 14th and baptized 15th July, 1780, married at Bradford, September, 1806, Thomas George Fitzgerald, of Co. Mayo, Ireland. Died December 9th, 1817. Buried at Oaklands.

John Wilmer Feild had two daughters: Mary, the elder, born July 21st, 1813, baptized at Bradford the 24th same, and christened September 8th following. Here the pedigree ends, but the author will add that she married on April 14th, 1836, Lord Oxmantown, afterwards Earl of Rosse. Delia, the younger daughter, was born October 23rd, 1814, baptized at Whitwell and christened at Bradford July 24th, 1815. She married the Honourable Arthur Duncombe, son of the first Baron Feversham, and afterwards Admiral and M.P. for East Riding of York.

Joshua Field and Elizabeth Wainman had also two daughters; Elizabeth, the elder, born July 13th, 1802, baptized at Bradford August 4th following. Died at Harrogate July 11th, 1822, and buried at Bradford. Mary Anne, the second daughter, was born February 19th, 1805, and died unmarried in 1825.

The descendants of Joseph Feild, lord of the manor of Heaton, baptized in 1601, became extinct in the male line, on the death of John Wilmer Feild and his brother

Joshua, neither of whom had a son, and their large estates at Bradford and in other parts of Yorkshire, passed out of the family. There may be male descendants of this Joseph Field's uncles, Thomas, William, or George ; but on this point the writer can give no information.

THE FIELDS OF OTHER PLACES IN
WAKEFIELD MANOR AND
NEIGHBOURHOOD.

N the subsidy roll ot 6th Henry VIII.
(1514-15), John Feyld is assessed under the
head of Sharleston, a place in the parish of
Warmfield, two or three miles south-east of
Wakefield. Among the wills at York is that of this same
person, "John Feld of Sharleston," dated June 28th,
1522, in which he desires " my bodie to be beried in the
chirche garthe of Warmfeld," and names in it his sons,
Henry, Lionell, and " Umfray," and his brother, Henry
Feld. Among the witnesses are Richard Feld and " John
Jobe (or Jube), senior." It was proved July 8th of
same year. In the subsidy roll of 15th Henry VIII.
(1523-24), Humfrey Feyld, Robert Feyld, and Richard
Feyld are assessed under the head of " Sharleston." On
April 18th, 1588, Robert Feild " of Sharleston in the
parish of Warmfeld," made his will, in which he mentions his wife Margaret, sister Janet, and daughters
Elizabeth, Agnes, Dorothy, Anne, and Jane. The will
of " Robert Feld of Croston ' (Cross-stone) in the parish
of Stansfield, husbandman," is dated May 7th, 1525. He
divides his property among his children, whom he does

' Crosstone, near Todmorden, and about half-a-dozen miles west of
Halifax.

not name. He mentions his brother, *i.e.*, brother-in-law, John Job, or Jub. It is witnessed by Brian Feld and Robert Feld, and was proved by his widow, Joan, and Thomas Feld, chaplain. The occurrence of the name of John Job, or Jub, in this last will, and in that of John Feld, of Sharleston, would seem to indicate a relationship between the testators, although the parishes of Stansfield and Warmfield are as far apart as any of the places named where the Fields were seated in the fifteenth and sixteenth centuries. The author would mention that the name "Jubbe" occurs in the visitation of Yorkshire of 1563-64. In 1604 John Feild, of Cross-stone, husbandman, names in his will his son Edmund, and daughters Frances Bourke, Jsabel, Anne, Susan, and Hester.

We find in the parish registers of Halifax the burials of Richard Feyld in 1540, Elizabeth Feyld in 1547, and of Edward Feld in 1551, all of that town. The will of another Richard Feild of Halifax, dated December 8th, 1557, and proved 22nd of same month, names his wife Ellen, and children Christopher, Robert, and Elizabeth; also a child unborn. The Halifax registers record the baptisms of Robert in 1552, Elizabeth in 1555, and Richard in 1558, all described as children of "Richard Fild," of Halifax.

In 1555 the marriage of Gilbert Feld and Isabella Harpur is recorded, and in the baptismal entries of their children, as below, he is described as of Halifax, viz., in 1556 "Sibil," 1557 Annis, 1560 Gilbert, and 1564 Johanna. Probably this last Gilbert is the person of that name mentioned in the Wakefield rolls in 1583 and 1592. In 1584 Frances, daughter of Richard Feld

I

of Halifax, was baptized, and in 1630 "Jonas, son of John Feild, of Halifax," buried.

In the Wakefield Manor rolls, under Alverthorpe, there is mention of land there in possession of John Feld in 1532 and of Roger Feild in 1607. In 1610 Roger and William Feild were tenants there, and in the following year "Roger Feild de Wakefield, chapman," took of the waste at Alverthorpe.

He is doubtless the Roger Feeld, against whom, in conjunction with Robert Smythe, a certain Leonard Foster brought an action, March 20th, 1599-60, as appears by the Duchy of Lancaster Pleadings; wishing to have these two removed from the custody of the daughters and lands of Roger Pollard, of Wakefield, deceased, on the ground that they were the next heirs. Feeld and Smythe reply that they are acting under Pollard's will, and that they are not the next heirs. In 1617 Roger Feild de Wakefield and Grace, his wife, are referred to under Alverthorpe, as ceding lands to John Maude, gent., of Wakefield, and in 1622 this Roger's lands there are spoken of.

Among the wills at York is that of Henry Feilde, "of Lexton, in the parish of Kirkheaton." He names his wife Isabel, his son-in-law John Beaumonte, and his "sister Thomas Naler's wife." It is dated February 28th, 1577-78, and was proved in the same year. His widow, Isabel, made hers on June 10th, 1583, and it was proved August 2nd of same year. She bequeaths all to her daughter Rosamond Beaumond.

William Feild of Newsome, in the parish of Almondbury, made his will November 1st, 1617. He mentions in it his sons William and George and daughter Rosa-

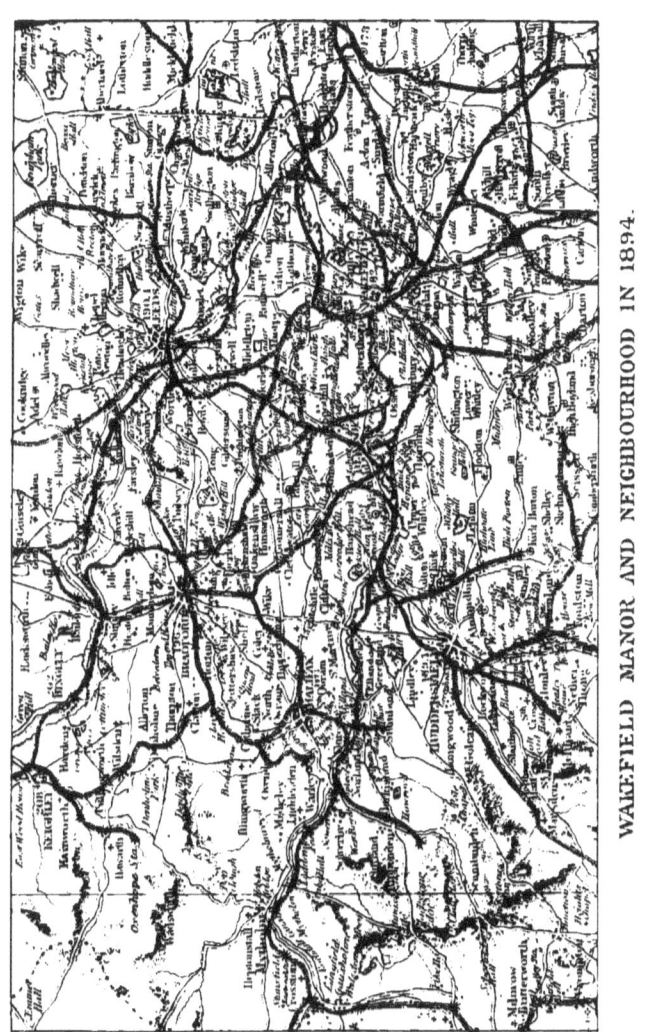

WAKEFIELD MANOR AND NEIGHBOURHOOD IN 1894.

mond, wife of Godfrey Kay,[1] also his grandson William, whose father was of same name.

It will be noticed that Henry and Isabel Feilde had a daughter Rosamond, named in the will of latter in 1583; and as we find that William of Newsome had also a daughter Rosamond, we may infer that the families were nearly related, more especially as they were residing in the same neighbourhood.

There are a few other notices of Fields in or near Wakefield Manor, among the author's papers, but the names mostly occur singly and possess no special interest.

[1] Some members of the ancient family of Key, or Kay, of Woodsome Hall, Almondbury, have claimed descent from Sir Kay, the knight of King Arthur's Round Table.

THE FIELDS OF FLUSHING, NEW YORK.

HE difficulty in the majority of American pedigrees, which attempt to trace back the family beyond the Atlantic, is to conneÆt the emigrant with the mother country and his ancestors there. In a few cases, an entry in some colonial record, a reference in an English or American will, a remark of one of the early historians of the New World, a letter or diary of the time still preserved, or one of the " passenger lists " of vessels sailing from the ports of London, Southampton, etc., for New England or Virginia (which often mentioned the old home of the emigrant), established this conneÆtion beyond question ; but these instances are rare, and in most cases there is only circumstantial evidence, more or less convincing, to prove it.

It is well known to those who are familiar with the law, that when a number of faÆts all point to one result, without anything contradiÆtory in them, the thing they indicate is often considered as well established, and many have suffered the penalty of death, on such evidence alone. The true genealogist, who reads this book, will probably ask, " What are the grounds for supposing that Robert Field, who was a patentee of Flushing, N.Y., in 1645, was the child who was baptized at Halifax, England, in 1605-6?" These reasons the author will now give, and he doubts not that they will satisfy the most critical.

It is well known to all students of our colonial history, that emigration to New England languished for ten years after the arrival there of the " Mayflower," and until the expedition was gotten up in 1630 by John Winthrop and Sir Richard Saltonstall, which embraced some 1,500 souls, who were transported to the other side of the Atlantic in seventeen ships, and arrived there in June or July of that year. All accounts agree that the friends and neighbours of the two leaders of the expedition contributed largely to swell its numbers. In the 8th of Elizabeth (1566) the Saltonstalls acquired by purchase a mansion called Rookes and lands at Hipperholme, which had descended to Sir Richard. He was living at this place, which adjoins Northowram, in 1630. Coley Chapel was built about 1500, by the united contributions of Hipperholme, Northowram, and Shelf, and the inhabitants of these three places were under its ministry. It follows that Sir Richard Saltonstall and Robert Field were neighbours, attending the same religious services, and probably friends.

The latter had no special ties in England. Both of his parents were dead; he was a younger son and single. He was twenty-four years old; an age when the spirit and love of adventure are strong in us, and nothing is more natural than that he should have accompanied Sir Richard to New England. They may have been connected; as Sir Richard's first wife was Grace, daughter of Robert Kay, Esq., of Woodsome, whom he married about 1609, and we have seen that William

Field of Newsome, who died in 1617, had a daughter Rosamond, wife of Godfrey Key, or Kay, the names being the same. The writer would mention, as a curious fact, that the first reference to a Field, who was beyond all question of the same family as this Robert, occurs in the Wakefield Manor rolls, in 1306, when Richard del Feld sued Robert de Saltonstall.

The early English settlements on Long Island were largely composed of emigrants from Yorkshire. In 1665, the year following the surrender of the colony by the Dutch to the English, a convention was held at Hempstead, when Long Island and Staten Island were erected into a shire, and called after that in England, Yorkshire. Like that, too, it was divided into a North Riding, East Riding, and West Riding.

Mr. Charles B. Moore says, in an article in "The New York Genealogical and Biographical Record," when speaking of the sixty-seven proprietors of land at Hempstead in 1647, that the European ancestry of many of these cannot be ascertained ; but that "at least ten of these men can be traced from Yorkshire, England. A much greater number doubtless came from that large county. So many came from Yorkshire that the settlement was characterized as a Yorkshire one."

At the time of the Winthrop and Saltonstall expedition the Rev. Richard Denton had been, since 1623, the officiating clergyman of Coley Chapel. In 1644 we find him among the first settlers of Hempstead, L.I. Thompson says of him, in his "History of Long Island," " It is quite probable that many of those who accompanied him here had belonged to his church in the mother country, and were determined to share his fortunes in a new region. Many of these emigrated with him to Watertown, Mass.," etc.

Nor was Denton the only one of his old friends and neighbours whom Robert Field found near him in his new home at Flushing ; for Matthew Mitchell, who was one of the witnesses of the will of his mother Susan in 1623, was also among the earliest settlers of Hempstead in 1644. Thompson says, in speaking of the first white inhabitants of this place, that Ward, Coe, and Mitchell were commissioners for Stamford. The Rev. Mr. Alvord wrote of them as follows : "They were among the earliest inhabitants of New England, coming, as we have seen, through Weathersfield from Watertown in Massachusetts, and *from that noted company who arrived with John Winthrop and Sir Richard Saltonstall.*" The Fields and Mitchells were connected by marriage, as already stated, for Robert's aunt Jane was married at Halifax, June 10th, 1622, to John " Michell," of Thornton. This couple are mentioned in the will of his mother, Susan Field, where the name is correctly spelt " Mitchell."

Among other early settlers in New England who were from the neighbourhood of Northowram, and who were connected with the Fields by marriage, were the Bairstows—sometimes spelt Barstow, Barrsto, or Beresto —and Jonathan Fairbanks. Thomas Feild and Susan Bairstow were married at Bradford on January 12th, 1618-19. Bond says, in his " History of Watertown," that four brothers of the name of Barstow, or Bairstow, came early to this country, viz., Michael, John, George, and William. In the passenger list of the " Freelove," sailing for New England, September 29th, 1635, are the names of William Beresto, aged twenty-three, and George Beresto, aged twenty-one years. Savage says that Michael was the eldest brother, and that he joined the Church December 5th, 1635. He adds, " *he was from Shelf, near Halifax, Co. York, West Riding.*" Not improbably Michael and John embarked first for the New World—perhaps in the expedition of 1630—and George and William followed a few years later.

On November 23rd, 1624, Robert Field and Ruth Fairebank, of Hipperholme, were married at Halifax. She was, without doubt, of the same family as Jonathan Fairbanks, of Dedham, who, Savage says, came to New England before 1641 with his wife Grace and probably all of his six children. Savage adds, "he was probably from the W. Riding of Yorkshire, as the will of his uncle George calls him *of Sowerby* in that part of England."

The Robert Field who married Ruth Fairebank was baptized at Halifax August 29th, 1602, when he is described as son of John Feelde, of Northowram. He is referred to in the Wakefield Manor rolls, the year of his marriage (1624), as holding lands at Hipperholme under Richard Sunderland. He had a son John, baptized at Halifax December 25th, 1625, who was buried there January 16th, 1625-26, being described on both occasions as " son of Robert Feild of Hipperholme."

There was another person of the same name as the settler at Flushing, who was also a contemporary. His name occurs in the " passenger list " of the " James," of London, which vessel sailed from Southampton for New England " about the VI. of April 1635."

He is entered on it as Robert Field, of Yealing (? Pealing, Berks), labourer." This Robert resided at

Boston, and had by his wife Mary, daughter of Christopher Stanley, twelve children, the eldest of whom, John, was baptized in 1644, and the youngest, Sarah, in 1665. Some accounts say that he was a tailor.

What became of the greater portion of those who went over with Winthrop and Saltonstall during the first few years of their stay in New England it is impossible to say, for so little documentary evidence exists of that period. It is known that a large proportion of the company went to Watertown on, or shortly after, their arrival, and Robert Field was probably one of these. He must have married soon after landing in America, for he had two sons of age in February, 1653-54. His wife, who survived him, was named Charity, and very probably she was one of the company that crossed the Atlantic with him, perhaps in the same ship. The author knows nothing of her family, and the only clue to it which he can offer, is that her second son had the rather unusual name of Anthony, and as this had not been borne by any of Robert's near relatives, it may have come from her side, and perhaps been that of her father.

The first notice of Robert Field in our colonial records occurs in the state of Rhode Island. It has been said of Roger Williams, who founded this colony, that he was " the first person in modern Christendom to assert in its plenitude the doctrine of liberty of conscience." In 1636 he fled from the religious tyranny and persecution of the New England Puritans, and founded the town to which he gave the name of Providence, in recognition of God's mercies. He was soon followed by others—residents of New England—

who are supposed to have shared his opinions, and among these was Robert Field.[1]

At a general meeting at Newport, R.I., held August 23rd, 1638, it was agreed "that 13 lots, on the west side of the spring, shall be granted to Mr. Richard Dummer and his friends," " to build there at the spring at farthest, or else their lots be disposed of by the company." Among the friends of Mr. Dummer we find Robert Field.

A little later the following entry occurs in the records : " Inhabitants admitted at the town of Newport, since the 20th of 3d (May), 1638." In this list are the names of Robert Field and John Hicks. On December 19th, 1639, Robert Field was made freeman of this town, and he is mentioned among the proprietors of land there in 1640. In the court roll of freemen, March 16th, 1641, are the names of Robert Field and John Hicks. This is the last time that the former is referred to in the records of Newport, except in 1653, when he visited the place, probably as delegate for Long Island, and he is not mentioned in the list of freemen of the town in 1655.

About the time of the settlement of Hempstead and Flushing, there was an intimate connection between the colony of Rhode Island and the English towns of Long Island. The inhabitants of both were mainly composed of the same class; viz., those who had fled from English persecution, and those who had escaped, like Roger Williams, from the no less intolerant Puritans of New

[1] John Field was one of eighteen persons desirous to inhabit the town of Providence, August 20th, 1636 or 1637, and he and William Field had house lots there in 1638. They may have been related to Robert, but the author has found no evidence of it.

England. We find many of the same names in both places at this early period of their history; not only those of Field and Hicks, but also Townsend, Hazard, Coles, and a number of others. We have seen that Robert Field and John Hicks are mentioned together more than once in the Newport records; and when we learn that they are again associated a little later, and are among the sixteen persons to whom the Dutch governor granted a patent for the town of Flushing, in 1645, we feel no moral doubt that the two settlers in Long Island were identical with the colonists of Rhode Island.

A further proof of this identity occurred a few years later. Governor Stuyvesant and the Dutch authorities at New Amsterdam, looked with a jealous eye on the inhabitants of the English towns within their jurisdiction; and, as a result of this feeling, the latter suffered many tyrannical and unjust acts at the hands of the government. The express stipulations of their charters were violated; illegal fines and taxes were imposed, and some were imprisoned or banished for their religious opinions. In 1653 an idea became prevalent among the inhabitants of these towns that the Dutch were inciting the Indians to a general massacre of the English, and supplying the savages with arms for that purpose. Probably their fears were exaggerated, but there is no doubt that the Dutch had some secret negotiations with the red men; with what object is not now known. It was whispered about that there was to be " a second Amboyna[1] tragedy; " and so great was the alarm, that

---

[1] Amboyna, one of the Moluccas, or Spice Islands, belonging to Holland. In 1623 an English settlement there (Cambello) was destroyed by the Dutch, and frightful tortures inflicted on the inhabitants.

many abandoned their homes and went to the colonies where they were under the protection of the English flag.

An application was made to Rhode Island for assistance, and probably Robert Field was one of those sent there to make the request, as he was specially qualified for this mission from having formerly resided in that colony, and being among old friends and neighbours there.   As we learn by the records, the deputation was successful.   At a general assembly held at Newport, May 18th, 1653, it was ordered that a committee be chosen " for refering matters that concern Long Island and in the case concerning the Dutch."   Eight members of this committee were selected, who were to " act upon presentment," and among these was " Mr. Robert Field." It was resolved at the same time " That we judge it our duty to afford our countrymen on Long Island what help we can," etc.   " That they shall have 2 great guns and what munitions are with us, etc. etc."

Captain John Underhill,[1] who had resided for some years on Long Island, was appointed commander of the forces by land, and Captain William Dyre of those by sea.

Under this commission, Captain Underhill captured the fort of Good Hope, near Hartford, from the Dutch in the month of June following.

How matters were arranged between the Government of New Amsterdam and their English subjects, is not exactly known ; probably steps were taken to convince the latter that their apprehensions of a general massacre were groundless, for those who had left Long Island returned to their homes shortly after, and matters resumed their old course.

[1] See Appendix.

The patent of the Governor-General of the New
Netherlands, William Kieft, was dated October 19th,
1645, and granted to Robert Field and his associates,
their heirs and assigns, " a certaine quantity, or parcell
of land, with all the Havens, Harbours, Rivers, Creekes,
Woodlands, Marshes thereunto belonging and being
upon the north side of Long Island," after which the
boundaries [1] are given.

Robert Field built his house at that part of Flushing
called Bayside. No trace of it exists, but family tradition says that it stood so near the water, that wild
ducks, while swimming on it, could be shot from the
porch.

Unfortunately for the historian of the first settlers of
Flushing, the town records were destroyed by fire in the
latter half of the last century; [2] but a few documents of
their time have come down to us, which have been
carefully preserved at the old Bowne house, built by
John Bowne in 1661. This ancient mansion is still
standing, and occupied by his descendants. From the time
of its erection, it was used by friends of the family and
neighbours as a depository for papers of value. Among
these is the following :

" February 12th, 1653 (*i.e.* 1653-4).

" Flushing. Know all men by these prēnts that I
Robert Field doe freely give and grant unto my two
sons Robert Field and Anthony Field each of them a

---

[1] See Appendix.

[2] These records were kept in the house of John Vanderbilt, the town
clerk. It was set fire to in October, 1789, and consumed with its con-
tents. Two slaves, Nelly and Sarah, were tried, condemned, and executed
for this crime.

house lott with the proprietie and priviledge thereunto
belonging. I give unto Robert the Lott w^h was formerly John Lake's. Unto Anthony the Lott which was
formerly given unto Thomas Aplegate's sones, which two
Lotts were purchased by mee and now freely are given
by mee unto them my two sones their heirs or assigns
forever to enjoy.

"ROBERT FIELD."

This document is important, as shewing that Robert
Field's two eldest sons were of age at the time it was
dated. The Thomas Applegate referred to in it was
also one of the original patentees of Flushing.

Robert Field, Robert Field, jun., and "Anthonie"
Field signed the petition to "the Governor Generall
and Counsell of the New Netherlands," in favour of the
"scoute," or sheriff of Flushing, William Hallett, who
was arrested for having religious meetings at his house.
There is no date to this petition, but it must have been
1656, for William Hallett was banished on November
8th of that year, and allowed to remain by a decree of
December 26th of same, on payment of a fine of £50
Flanders, and at same time deprived of his office.

All three of the Fields signed the bold remonstrance[1]
against the persecution of Quakers, addressed to the
Governor-General, and dated December 27th, 1657.

In the examination of Edward Hart, in reply to the
question, " Who signed at the meeting and who at their
houses ? " he said, " Anthony Field, and both of ye Fields
(*i.e.* Robert sen. and jun.), at ye house of ye village black-
smith, Michael Milner," where the meeting was held.

---

[1] This document will be found in Thompson's "History of Long
Island," vol. ii., p. 289.

This remonstrance bore the signatures of thirty of the principal inhabitants of the town, and the whole tenor of it shews that they were in advance of the age in their views in regard to religious freedom and liberty of conscience. Tobias Feake,[1] the sheriff, who presented the paper, was immediately arrested. Hart, who drew it up, and Farrington and Noble, two of the magistrates who signed it, were imprisoned.

A patent of confirmation of Flushing, dated February 16th, 1666, names but one Robert Field, who is styled neither "senior" nor "junior." It follows that either the emigrant was dead, or that his son Robert had left Flushing. The author inclines to the latter opinion, as we know that the younger Robert was at Newtown in or before 1670, where he resided for the rest of his life and died.

His father, however, was no longer living in 1673, as shewn in the following document, preserved at the old Bowne house, which also establishes the name of his wife :

"February y⁶ 6ᵗʰ 1672 (*i.e.* 1672-3).

" Know all men by these prĕnts that I Charity Field, widow, Doe own and Confess that the home Lott that Lyeth betwixt the Lott that was formerly old Applegate's, and the Lott that was formerly . . . . Doughty's is my sone Anthony Field's Lott and proper land, and I never intended nor pretended any right to it.

"Testes   "Witness my hand
" Elias Doughty " Charity Field."
" Robert Field."

<hr>

[1] Son of Robert Feake, of Watertown, Mass.

She is also referred to in a letter from John Bowne to his wife, written while he was abroad, and dated, " Amsterdam this 9ᵗʰ of the 4ᵗʰ mo. called June 1663."

The passage reads as follows : " Remember my true love to Joan Chatterton and Charity Field."

Robert Field, junior, was probably the eldest son, as he is the first named in the deed of 1653-4. As already stated, he removed to the adjoining town of Newtown in or before 1670. He appears in the records of that place as selling land there in 1671. He was one of the two overseers of Newtown in 1672, 1674, 1675, 1678, and 1680.

In the valuation of estates there in 1675, Robert Field had " 30 acres of land, 1 horse, 2 oxen, 5 cows, 3 three year olds, 2 two year olds, 1 one year old, twenty sheep and 2 swine, one male person." I infer from the last sentence that all his sons were then under age. In 1683 Robert Field and Robert Field, jun., were ratepayers at Newtown, and in 1685 the names of both are in a list of residents, and probably freeholders there. On November 25th, 1686, Governor Dongan granted a new patent to the inhabitants of Newtown, confirming their rights, which mentions both Roberts. We learn by the records of Queen's County, Long Island, that Robert Field, sen., of Newtown, on October 8th, 1690, gave to his son Nathaniel Field lands and salt meadows at the head of the " ffly " at Flushing. If he died without " heires," to go to his brother Elnathan. Attested before Elias Doughty, Justice, May 26th, 1691. On same day Robert gave to his son Benjamin his homestead at Newtown, and "in case he has no heirs to go to his brother Ambrose." In the Friends' records, under fourth month, 1699-1700, "Susannah Field of New-town, daughter of Robert Field," and Isaac Marit (? Merritt), of Burlington, West Jersey, declared intention of marriage.

We learn also by the Flushing records of the Society of Friends that Robert Field, of Newtown, died the 13th day of the second month, 1701. The writer is inclined to put the date of his birth as 1631. This accords with what Mr. James Riker, the historian of Newtown, wrote to him, " Robert, senʳ, at his death in 1701, could not have been less than 65 to 70 years of age." His wife, whose name was Susannah, survived him.

Anthony Field, son of the emigrant, and probably the second child, remained at Flushing. We have seen that his father deeded a house lot to him in 1653-4, and that he signed public documents of some importance in 1656 and 1657. He is named in the patent of confirma-tion of Flushing in 1666, and also among those who took the oath of allegiance in 1673.

A valuation of estates at Flushing was made in 1675, which has the following entry : " Anthony Felde, 27 acres, 2 horses, 2 oxen and 5 cows." His name occurs in a similar document in 1683 as follows : " Anthony Feild, 50 acres, 2 oxen, 4 cows, 4 swine, 10 sheep." From 1675 to 1683 he was among the ratepayers of Flushing, and he is one of those to whom a patent of confirmation of that town was granted, March 23rd, 1685. This is the last occasion on which the author finds him mentioned, and he died before his son Benjamin married in 1691, as he is spoken of in the entry of it as " deceased." We know from this record that his wife,

L

who survived him, was named Susannah, but that of her family has not come down to us. We also learn from it that Benjamin was not his only son.

Benjamin Field, presumably the third son of the emigrant, was appointed ensign for Flushing by Nicoll, the Governor of New York, on April 22nd, 1665. He is named in the Flushing patents of February 16th, 1666, and of 1685, and was a juror at the Court of Assizes in 1669. On March 22nd, 1671, he conveyed by deed to John Bowne his "two shares of fresh meadows, being Nos. 34 and 42." His death is recorded as follows in the register of the Society of Friends of Flushing: "Benjamin Field of Flushing, an antient friend, dyed the 1st of the 10th mo. 1732." His age must have been at least between eighty-seven and ninety. He left a widow, Sarah, whose will was dated the 26th of ninth month, 1732, only a few days before her husband died, but it appears from the register referred to that she survived him. The entry of her death is as follows: "Sarah Field, widow of Benjamin Field of Flushing, dyed 1734." The day and month are not given; but it must have been early in 1734, as her will was proved March 20th of that year. She styles herself in it "wife of Benjamin Field of Flushing," and appoints him one of her executors, another being her grandson, William Doughty. Two other grandsons are mentioned—William March and Henry March. Apparently Benjamin and Sarah Field left no male descendants. Robert Field, of Newtown, grandson of the emigrant, married Phœbe, daughter of Edmond Titus, and widow of . . . Scudder. The register of the Society of Friends says, in an entry referring to her father's death, that " his daughter Pheby

Field, standing by him, he . . . . departed this life in a quiet frame of spirit sensible to the last, the 7th 2^d mo. 1715,—aged 85."

Her marriage is entered as follows in the Friends' register : "Robert Field son of Robert Field of New-town and Phebe Scudder of Westbury 24th day of 12th mo. 1689, at the house of Edmond Titus of West-bury."

This Robert Field's will was dated the 10th day of the 10th month, 1734, and proved April 16th, 1735. He names in it his brother Elnathan's children, Robert, Benjamin, Susannah, Phœbe, and Mary ; the daughters of his brother Nathaniel, who are not named, and a daughter of his brother Ambrose, also not named. There are bequests to his sister Susannah, wife of Peter Thorne, to Robert Field and wife Elizabeth, and " my cousin (*i.e.* nephew) Robert Field " is one of the executors. His widow, Phœbe, made her will the 12th day of the 11th month, 1742. There are numerous legacies in it to relatives and friends, and among others to the wife of Robert Field and her two daughters and two sons, Elnathan and Robert. It is evident from their wills that Robert and Phœbe Field died childless.

Elnathan Field, of Newtown, brother of the last Robert, made his will July 12th, 1735. He mentions in it his wife Elizabeth, his eldest son Robert, son Benjamin, and his daughters Susannah, Sackett, and Phœbe and Mary Coe. The author supposes that he survived some time after the date of it, as it was not proved till February 7th, 1754. An earlier entry in the Friends' register records the birth of some of his children thus, the date of it being uncertain :

"*Children of Elnathan and Elizabeth Field.*
Elizabeth, born the 24ᵗʰ day of 4ᵗʰ mo. 1696.
Robert,   „   12ᵗʰ   „   3ᵈ „ 1698.
Elnathan,   „   19ᵗʰ   „   9ᵗʰ „ 1700."

In all probability Elizabeth and Elnathan died before the wills of their father and uncle Robert were made, and their brother Benjamin and sisters were not born at the date of this entry in the register.

Nathaniel Field, brother of Robert, third of the name, and of Elnathan, married, the 9th day of the 5th month, 1701, Patience Bull, "formerly of Bermudas." The author can give no further account of him, nor of his brother Ambrose, who was one of the witnesses of his marriage. As shewn in their brother Robert's will, Nathaniel had daughters and Ambrose a daughter in 1734. There may be descendants living of these two, and their brother Elnathan, but the author has not the means of tracing them.

The following entry in the Flushing register of the Society of Friends relates to the remaining son of Robert and Susannah Field: "Benjamin Field and Experience Allen declare intentions of marriage 29ᵗʰ 6ᵗʰ mo. 1692." Such declarations were common in the society of which they were members. As the marriage is not recorded in the Flushing registers, the writer presumes that it took place elsewhere.

Miss Annis S. Field, of Princeton, New Jersey, daughter of the late Hon. Richard S. Field, wrote to the author on June 24th, 1875: "I have examined an old family bible in the possession of my aunt and have copied for you the record, just as it stands." It is as follows :

" Robert Field, son to Benjamin and Experience Allen, was born the 6th of January, 1694.

" Mary Field, daughter to Samuel and Susanna Taylor, was born the 31st of March, 1700.

" Robert Field, son to the above Robert and Mary Field, was born the 9th May, 1723.

" Susannah Field, daughter to Robert and Mary Field, was born the 21st February, 1730.

" Samuel Field, son to the above Robert and Mary, was born Feby., 1736.

(Two other children, names torn off.)

" Robert Field, son to Robert and Mary, married Mary, daughter of Oswald and Lydia Peale.

" *Children of the Above.*

Lydia, born 10th of October, 1766.
Mary,   ,,   ,,   ,,   ,,
Robert, ,, July 10th, 1769.
Grace, ,, Oct. 10th, 1770.
Susan, ,, Apl. 20th, 1772.
Samuel, ,, July 14th, 1773.
Robert, ,, April 5th, 1775."

Miss Field adds in her letter : " The Robert last named was my grandfather. All the other children died in infancy."

The writer will add that the Robert who married Mary Peale died January 29th, 1775. His posthumous son of same name, born a few months after his father's death, married, in 1797, Abby, daughter of Richard Stockton and Annis Boudinot. He died in 1810, leaving five children, among whom was the Hon. Richard Stockton Field, sometime senator for New Jersey. He married Miss Mary Ritchie, and died May 25th, 1870, leaving three children to survive him.

The author is somewhat at a loss where to place a John Field, who was at Flushing at an early period. There is a person of this name among those who took the oath of allegiance in a list without date, and with no place named.

As the province of New York was definitely ceded by the Dutch to the English in 1674, he does not think that it could have been later.

There is also among the Albany records an entry referring to a tract of land granted by Governor Andros to John Field. No date is mentioned, but it must have been between 1674 and 1681, which years embrace Andros' tenure of this office.

The record commences : " Whereas there is a certain parcel of land, which by my order hath been laid out for John Field, called by the name of Field's Hope, situated in a creek called Maspillan Creek, and on the east side of said creek, and on the west side of Delaware Bay, etc., etc., etc."

In the valuation of estates at Flushing in 1683, John Field had " 5 acres, 2 cowes, and 4 swine." He is named in the patent of confirmation of this town in 1685. The records of the Society of Friends at Flushing are pretty complete from about this date, and there are the names of a number of witnesses to every later marriage of a member of the family, but his does not appear among them. The author infers that he either died, or left the neighbourhood, in or shortly after

1685. In the latter case he may have been the grantee of "Field's Hope," and removed there.

The American Bible Society possesses an old bible presented to it by the Hon. Peter D. Vroom, of Trenton, New Jersey, which has the following :

"Jeremiah Feild, the son of John Field and Margaret his wife, was born May 17th, 1689.

"Mary Van Veghten, the daughter of Michael Van Veghten and Mary his wife, was born Oct. 8th, 1687. Jeremiah Feild and Mary Van Veghten (widow of Albert Tencick) were married Feby. 19th, 1712-13. Their children were :

"Jeremiah, born Jany. 27th, 1713-14.
John   „   Apl. 5th, 1715.
Michael   „   Aug. 24th, 1716.
Margaret   ,,   Oct. 2d, 1717.
Mary   „   Sep. 8th, 1719.
Mary   „   Oct. 19th, 1720.
Michael   ,,   Feby. 4th, 1722-3.
Benjamin   ,,   Feby. 19th, 1724-5.

"Father Jeremiah, deceased, Nov. 10, 1746.

"Jeremiah Field, Jr., and Phœbe his wife, their daughter, born Jany. 19th, 1736.

"Tunes Field, son of Jeremiah Field, was married to Margaret Fisher, March 28, 1764."

John Field, of Flushing, must have been the son of the emigrant, or his grandson and son of Anthony. If he took an oath of allegiance as early as 1674, or had a grant of land within a year or two of that date, he could hardly have been the son of Anthony, whose birth the author would place in 1631, 1632, or 1633.

He supposes that the John Field who had a grant of land on Delaware Bay was the father of Jeremiah, and not unlikely that all the references given refer to the same individual, and he a younger son of the emigrant.

It was probably after the death of the emigrant, and during the lifetime of his sons, that the family became members of the Society of Friends. It is pretty evident that they had not joined it when Benjamin was appointed ensign in 1665, considering that the society does not allow its members to undertake military duties. George Fox, who is looked upon by many as the real founder of this sect, visited Flushing in 1672, and, while there, was the guest of John Bowne at the old mansion already referred to. Meetings of the members were held—first at this house, and afterwards in the open air, sometimes in the woods, and secretly, on account of the persecutions to which they were exposed. Fox is represented to have been a man possessing great natural eloquence, and under his preaching the leading inhabitants of Flushing and neighbourhood became Friends, and among these, probably, the Fields, most of whom continued to be members of the society for nearly a century and a half, while some are at the present day.

In the Friends' records of Flushing the names of Joseph and Thomas Field are among those who witnessed a marriage in 1700. There is no later mention in them of Joseph, but Thomas was a witness on a similar occasion in 1718. It would appear from the entry of this Thomas's death, that he was born about 1674. Both he and Joseph are named in a list of the inhabitants of Flushing in 1698, and described in it as "single men."

Thomas could hardly have been the son of the first settler Robert, who had probably been dead more than a year in 1674; nor the son of Robert of Newtown, whose deeds of land to his sons in 1690, as also the will of the third Robert in 1734, do not mention him. Neither could he have been the son of Anthony, as Benjamin, the "youngest son" of the last, was married in 1691. There is very little doubt but that he was a grandson of Robert, who was patentee of Flushing in 1645, but the author cannot say who was his father. Reference will be made to this Thomas hereafter.

Among other papers preserved at the old Bowne house is the draft of the following letter from Hannah Bowne to her parents. It bears no date, but was no doubt written in 1690, for in that year her father lost his second wife, Hannah Bickerstaffe, and did not marry his third, Mary Cock, till 1693 : " And dear father and mother, I may also acquaint you that one Benjamin Field, the youngest son of my friend Susannah Field, has tendered his love to me,—the question he has indeed proposed as concerning marriage the which as yet I have not at present rejected nor given much way to nor do I intend to proceed nor let out my affection too much towards him till I have well considered the thing and have your's and friends' advice and consent concerning it."

The writer of this letter was Hannah, daughter of John Bowne,[1] and his first wife Hannah, daughter of Robert Feaks,[2] or Feeks, as it was sometimes spelt. This Feaks married Elizabeth Fones, granddaughter of

[1] See Appendix.   [2] See Appendix.

M

Adam Winthrop, of Groton, and widow of her cousin Henry, son of John Winthrop, first Governor of Massachusetts. Hannah Bowne was born in 1665, according to the Friends' register, and her marriage entry in it occurs the year after the supposed date of her letter. It reads : " Benj Field son of Anthony Field of Long Island deceased and Hannah Bowne daughter of John Bowne of Long Island aforesaid married 30th 9th 1691 at John Bowne's in Flushing."

At the old Bowne house is a deed of land by Benjamin Field to Samuel Bowne, dated 9th, 12th month, 1696-7. In a list of the inhabitants of Flushing in 1698 is the following : " Benj Feild and Hannah his wife, children Benj, John, Anthony and Sam'l, negroes Jo and Betty."

At the old Bowne house two or three letters are preserved, dated at Chesterfield in 1700 and 1701, signed B. Field, and addressed to Samuel Bowne. They relate, to purchases of land in that neighbourhood, in which they were both interested. One of them speaks of " another purchase of land to the quantity of 1000 to 1500 acres," which " lyes above the falls of Delaware, about 10 or 11 miles from Salem."

This Samuel Bowne was son of John and Hannah, and born in 1667. It has been stated that there were three Benjamin Fields living at the date of these letters ; but they were doubtless written by the son of Anthony, who was the brother-in-law of the person to whom they were addressed. One of them commences, " Dear and loving friend and *kinsman* Samuel Bowne."

The following entry is in the register of the Flushing Friends :

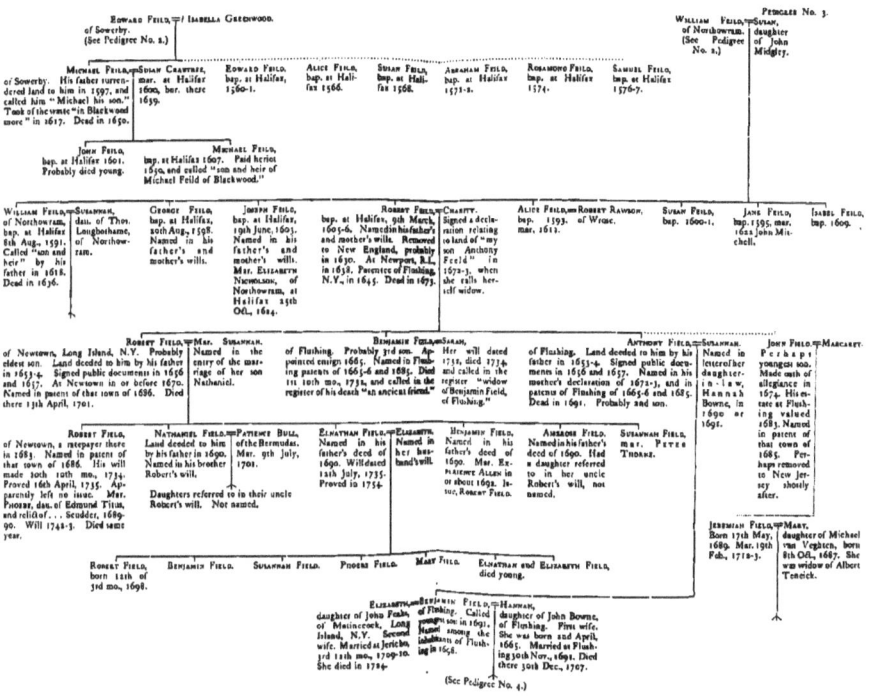

" *Children of Benjamin and Hannah Field.*

Benjamin,	born	5th day,	12th mo.	1692.
John,	,,	13th ,,	11th ,,	1694.
Samuel,	,,	10th ,,	8th ,,	1696.
Anthony,	,,	28th ,,	5th ,,	1698.
Hannah,	,,	20th ,,	5th ,,	1700.
Joseph,	,,	12th ,,	4th ,,	1702.
Sarah,	,,	17th ,,	6th ,,	1704.
Robert,	,,	7th ,,	7th ,,	1707."

Hannah Field died shortly after the birth of the last child, as shewn by this entry : " Hannah Field wife of Benjamin Field of Flushing died 30th day 10th mo. 1707." Her husband married again a lady who must have been a near relative of his first wife and her mother. This marriage is thus entered in the register : " Benjamin Field and Elizabeth Feaks, daughter of John Feaks of Matinecock, married the 3d day of 12th mo. 1709-10, at Jericho." Her death is recorded as follows : " Elizabeth Field wife of Benjamin Field of Flushing died 1724." As far as the writer can learn, she left no children, nor does he know the date of her husband's death.

The marriages of several of the children of Benjamin Field and Hannah Bowne are recorded in the Friends' register of Flushing, as follows :

" Samuel Field, son of Benjamin Field and Mary Palmer, daughter of William Palmer, married at Flushing 7th day of 1st mo. 1718."

" John Field, son of Benjamin Field, and Elizabeth Woolsey, daughter of John Woolsey, married 12th day of 11th mo. 1720, at Flushing."

" Thomas Heaviland, son of Benjamin Heaviland and

Hannah Field, daughter of Benjamin Field, at Flushing, 9th day of 1st mo. 1721."

" Robert Field, son of Benjamin Field of Flushing and Rebecca Burling, daughter of William Burling of same place, married 13th of 9th mo. 1729."

" Anthony Field, son of Benjamin Field of Flushing and Hannah Burling, daughter of William Burling, of the same place, married the 13th day of 6th mo. 1730 at the meeting house Flushing."

The author supposes that the Benjamin Field of the next entry was the son of Benjamin and Hannah, who was born in 1692.

" Benjamin Field of Flushing and Sarah Tayler of same place married 13th day of 2^d mo. 1727, at Flushing."

The writer has found among his papers a memorandum giving some of the descendants of Benjamin Field and Hannah Bowne, but he is unable to give his authority for the statements in this paper.   They are as follows :

" Samuel Field and Mary Palmer had sons William, John and Stephen.

" William, the first named of these 3 children, had William and Samuel.

" Joseph, another son of Benjamin and Hannah, had Comfort, Gilbert, Nehemiah and Solomon.

" Robert, youngest son of Benjamin and Hannah had Sarah, Uriah and Jerusha.

" Uriah, only son of Robert, had Aaron, Abigail, Elizabeth, Robert, Josiah, Hannah, James, Sarah, Mary, and Anna.

" Aaron, the first named of Uriah's children, had Charles, Richard, Sarah, Anna, Eliza, and Hannah.

" Charles, son of Aaron, had Phœbe, Jane, Edward, Richard, Charles M. Louisa M. and Aaron."

Reference will be made hereafter to Anthony, son of Benjamin Field, who married Hannah Burling in 1730.

Thomas Field, who was named among the inhabitants of Flushing in 1698, and was then single, had the following issue according to the Friends' register:

" *Children of Thomas and Hannah Field.*

William born 22^d day 10th mo. 1701.
Nathan   ,,   30th ,,   9th ,,   1703.
Caleb   ,,   5th ,,   11th ,,   1705.
Jacob   ,,   23^d ,,   5th ,,   1708.
Mary   ,,   30th ,,   10th ,,   1710.
Sarah   ,,   6th ,,   7th ,,   1712.
Hannah   ,,   27th ,,   5th ,,   1715.
Thomas   ,,   28th ,,   9th ,,   1719.
Joseph   ,,   29th ,,   2^d ,,   1722."

The marriages of some of these children are entered in the Flushing registers, viz. :

On the 10th of the 12th month, 1725-6, Nathan Field, " son of Thomas and Hannah Field of Flushing," and Elizabeth Jackson, daughter of James and Rebecca Jackson were married.

" John Clarke and Sarah Field, daughter of Thomas of Flushing were married 3^d day of 2^d mo. 1735."

" Joseph Field, son of Thomas and Hannah and Mary Rodman, daughter of Thomas and Elizabeth, married the 16th of 6th 1750."

The last couple had a son Rodman Field, born on the

2nd day of 8th mo., 1751. The mother, Mary Field, died 23rd of same month, "aged about 22."

Caleb Field, son of Thomas and Hannah, married Anne Rodman, who was probably a sister of his brother Joseph's wife. They had Thomas, born 28th of 7th mo., 1747, and, probably, Elizabeth, Mary, who married Walter Farrington; Anna, who married John Bowne, and Philip.

Thomas, son of Thomas and Hannah Field, died 9th of 10th mo., 1748; and the eldest of the brothers, William, the 4th of 3rd mo., 1759.

The death of the father of these children is entered in the registers as follows: "Thomas Field deceased the 3rd day of 1st mo. 1761 aged about 87." This would make the date of his birth about 1674. His wife's death is recorded immediately after, thus: "Hannah Field, his widdow, died the 2d day of 2d mo. 1761, aged about 81. They had been married and lived together near sixty years."

The author has already stated that he is unable to say who was the father of this Thomas. The most plausible suggestion he can offer is, that he was son of Benjamin Field, the son of the emigrant who was appointed ensign for Flushing in 1665, and by a first wife. It is pretty evident from the will of his widow Sarah, that she left no child; but she may have been the second wife, and perhaps her husband had issue by a previous one.

Anthony Field, son of Benjamin and Hannah, who was born in 1698 and married Hannah Burling,[1] removed to Harrison, sometimes called "Harrison's Purchase" and sometimes "Purchase" in 1725.

[1] See Appendix.

This tract was bought from the Indians by John
Harrison, of Flushing, to whom it was conveyed by
a deed of Pathungo, sachem, or chief of the tribe residing there, dated 24th January, 1695. It is in the
county of Westchester and about thirty miles from New
York. Originally it formed part of Rye, but was
separated from it after the Indian deed referred to, and
successfully resisted the claims of ownership made by this
town. Bolton, the historian of Westchester, says,
"Nearly all the settlers of this purchase came from
Flushing and other towns on Long Island." And
again, " This seems to have been a favourite settlement
of the Friends. They were shamefully persecuted in
Connecticut and Massachusetts; from there driven to
Long Island. Even there they could find no rest, for the
Governor of New York issued an order forbidding them
to worship, even in a barn. So they crossed by means of
the ferry to Rye and settled principally in Harrison."
Anthony Field gave the ground for the first Friends'
meeting house erected here in 1727, which land ad-
joined his estate.

His will was dated, " this twenty-first day of the
fourth month (called April), 1773." After providing for
his wife Hannah, he directs his land to be sold " that
lies on the North side of the road that leads from King
street to White Plains ; " and out of the proceeds certain
sums to be paid to his sons Thomas, Samuel, Anthony,
and John, " which will make them equal with what my
son Benjamin hath already had, which is eighty pounds; "
also forty pounds to son William and the same sum to
daughter Sarah out of the said proceeds, and the remainder of same to be equally divided between his children

Thomas, William, and Sarah. "When my widdow pleases to sell the farm, where I now live on the East side of the road that leads from the Purchase meeting house to Rye," eighty pounds is to be paid "to my son Moses Field," the remainder to be divided equally between his—the testator's—"widdow" and his children, except Anthony, who has had his full share. His land in Hampshire (*i.e.* New Hampshire), is to be equally divided between his sons William and Moses. "My beloved wife Hannah Field and my sons Benjamin and John Field to be executors." His death is entered as follows in the Friends' register of Harrison : "Anthony Field died 9th mo. 2d 1777," and he was interred in the burial ground of the meeting house there.

Of the children of Anthony Field and Hannah, Benjamin married Jerusha Sutton ; William married Mary Hatfield ; Anthony married Mary French ; Samuel married Abigail Haight ; and Sarah married Joseph Waters. Another son, John, who was one of his father's executors, married Lydia Hazard. Their union is recorded in the Friends' register of Newport, Rhode Island, as follows :

"John Field of the purchase in the County of Westchester in the province of New York, son of Anthony and Hannah Field and Lydia Hazard, daughter of William Hazard [1] and Phœbe his wife of Jamestown married 8th of 6th 1763 at the meeting house in Jamestown."

John Field removed from Harrison to Yorktown, which is also in Westchester county, and lies a few miles back of Peekskill, and died there in 1815. The death

[1] See Appendix.

of his wife Lydia occurred January 15th, 1795. Their children were Hazard Field, born November 11th, 1764, married Fanny Wright in June, 1778, by whom he had Rachel, who married Jonathan Hart; Hannah, married William McCord; Wright, married Phœbe Anne Drake, and Sarah Anne, married Elias Vredenburgh. Hazard Field married secondly, January 12th, 1806, Mary Bailey, by whom he had Fanny Field, married Elias Vredenburgh, whose first wife was her half sister; Abigail, died single; Susan, died single; Phœbe, married Jacob McCord; Benjamin Hazard, married Catharine van Cortlandt de Peyster; Joseph Bailey, died single and Jerusha M. died single; John Field, second child of John and Lydia, born May 6th, 1766, married Fanny Perry, and had Josiah A., married Eliza Holsted; Edward married Eliza Morrin; Ira died an infant; James P. Stephen, married Frances Bouton Kellogg. A daughter, married to George Merrill; Elizabeth, married Reuben Kellogg; Maria, married G. B. Rolleston; Harriet; John, married Eleanor Hardie; William, married A. Beach; Louisa, married Charles H. Culyer; and Walter, married Melinah Truesdell.

Josiah Field, third child of John and Lydia, died single, February 27th, 1806. Daniel Birdsall Field, fourth child of John and Lydia, born July 28th, 1770, married Elizabeth, daughter of Benjamin Field, and had Leonard Hungerford Field, married Margaret Clement; Juliet, married Frederick William Requa; James Harvey, married Jeanne Charlotte Victoria Dubourg; and Eliza, who died single.

Abigail Field, fifth child of John and Lydia, died in infancy.

N

James Field, sixth child of John and Lydia, died in infancy.

Sarah Field, seventh child of John and Lydia, born August 7th, 1775, married Caleb Horton.

William B. Field, eighth child of John and Lydia, born December 2nd, 1777, married . . . . Fairchild, and had William H. Field, married Margaretta Day.

Moses Field, ninth child of John and Lydia, was father of the author, and will be referred to after all their other children.

Abigail Field, tenth child of John and Lydia, was born January 16th, 1782, and died young.

Phœbe Field, eleventh child of John and Lydia, was born January 16th, 1784, and married Henry Fowler.

Jerusha Field, twelfth child of John and Lydia, was born March 14th, 1786, and died single, December 28th, 1877.

Hickson Woolman Field,[1] thirteenth child of John and Lydia, was born October 17th, 1788, married Eleanor, daughter of William de Forrest, by whom he had Hickson W. Field, who married Mary Elizabeth, daughter of John Maunsell Bradhurst, and Eleanor Kingsland, who married Hon. John Jay. H. W. Field, the father, married secondly, Catharine, daughter of Samuel Bradhurst, and died at Rome, February 12th, 1873.

Samuel Field, fourteenth child of John and Lydia, died in infancy.

Seaman Field, fifteenth child of John and Lydia, was born February 3rd, 1793, and married Louise Marie Eliza

[1] See Appendix.

Dubourg, of Louisiana, by whom he had Marie Eliza-
beth Wilhelmine, who died in infancy; Joseph de Forrest,
died single; Charles Victor de Gournay, died young.
Jeanne Eliza, married Theodore Bailly Blanchard;
Louise Augustine Odile, married William Hazard
Vredenburgh; Henry William Dubourg died in infancy;
Marie Clemence, married James Arthur Blanc; and
Elizabeth Victoire, who died in infancy.

James Field, sixteenth child of John and Lydia, born
January 15th, 1795, died in infancy.

Moses Field, ninth child of John and Lydia, and
named after an uncle, was born October 4th, 1779. He
removed to New York about 1800, where his elder
brother Josiah had already preceded him, and had been
associated in business with John Maunsell Bradhurst.
After Josiah's death Moses Field became a member of
the firm of Bradhurst and Field, merchants, from which
he retired in or before 1820, and shortly after made the
usual European tour, visiting England, France, Italy,
etc. On May 17th, 1821, not long after his return to
America, he married Susan Kittredge, daughter of the
Hon. Samuel Osgood,[1] First Commissioner United
States Treasury, Postmaster-General under Washington's
administration, etc. She was born April 12th, 1795.

Moses Field had the following children :

Maunsell Bradhurst,[2] born March 26th, 1822, who
married Julia, daughter of Daniel Stanton. He was
Assistant Secretary of the Treasury under Lincoln's
administration, and afterwards Judge of the Second District Court of New York. Died 1875.

Osgood Field, the second child, and author of this

[1] See Appendix.   [2] See Appendix.

book, was born November 14th, 1823. He resided for some years in London and afterwards in Rome. On October 7th, 1880, he married Katharine Roxana, daughter of Milton Day Parker, of Utica, New York.

Franklin Clinton Field, the third child, was born August 5th, 1825. He married first, Mary, daughter of William Cunningham, December 18th, 1861, and secondly, Elizabeth Cooke, daughter of George Fitch, January 30th, 1872.

Susan Maria, the fourth child, married John Augustus Pell. She was born August 13th, 1827, and died at Pau, France, December 30th, 1893.

Caroline Matilda, fifth child, born March 11th, 1829, married George S. Riggs of Baltimore.

Moses Augustus, sixth child, born April 15th, 1831, married March 16th, 1854, Fanny Pearsall, daughter of Samuel Bradhurst.

William Hazard, youngest child, born August 5th, 1833, married October 15th, 1863, Augusta Currie, daughter of Samuel Bradhurst.

Moses Field[1] died at Peekskill, N.Y., on October 21st, 1833, after a life of unostentatious benevolence. During the severe winter of 1828-9, when there was much suffering among the poor of New York, he established a soup house, and kept it up at his own expense, with the exception of some small sums, which were sent to him unsolicited on his part. The writer— then quite a child—can remember being taken by him on several occasions to this place, where a good meal was given to all the necessitous who came there, and he

[1] See Appendix.

ELIZABETH, ⚭ BENJAMIN FIELD, ⚭ HANNAH, dau. of
dau. of John of Flushing. (See John Bowne, 1st
Peaks, 2nd wife. Pedigree No. 3.) wife.

| BENJAMIN FIELD, born 5th 12th mo., 1692. Mar. SARAH TAYLOR, 13th 2nd mo., 1727. | JOHN FIELD, ⚭ born 13th 11th mo., 1694-5. died 1773. Mar. ELIZABETH, dau. of John Woolsey, 12th 11th mo., 1720. | SAMUEL FIELD, born 10th 8th mo., 1696. Mar. MARY, dau. of Wm. Palmer, 7th 1st mo., 1718. | ANTHONY FIELD, ⚭ HANNAH, born 28th 5th mo., dau. of Wm. 1698, of Harrison, Burling, of West. Co., N.Y., Flushing, mar. to which place he 13th 6th mo., removed in 1725. 1730. Survived Will dated 21st her husband. April, 1773. Died 2nd 9th mo., 1777. | ROBT. FIELD, ⚭ born 7th 7th mo., 1707. Mar. REBECCA, dau. of Wm. Burling. | HANNAH FIELD, born 20th 5th mo., 1700. Mar. THOS. HAVILAND. | JOSEPH FIELD, born 13th 4th mo., 1701. Left issue. | SARAH FIELD, born 17th 6th mo., 1704. |

| WILLIAM FIELD. Mar. MARY HATFIELD. | ANTHONY FIELD. Mar. MARY FRENCH. | JOHN FIELD, ⚭ LYDIA, of Yorktown, dau. of Wm. West. Co., N.Y., Hazard, of James-born 1731. Died town, R.I. Mar. in 1815. father's will. Died 12th executor of his 1763. Died 13th father's will. Jan., 1795. | BENJAMIN FIELD. Mar. JERUSHA SUTTON. | SAMUEL FIELD. Mar. ABIGAIL HAIGHT. | SARAH FIELD. Mar. JOSEPH WATERS. | THOMAS MOSES FIELD. Mar. MARY FIELD. | } Died in infancy. |

| HAZARD FIELD, ⚭ of Yorktown, born 11th Nov., 1764, died 5th 1st, FANNY WRIGHT ; and, MARY BAILAY. | JOHN FIELD, ⚭ born 6th May, 1766. Mar. FANNY PERRY. | DANIEL FIELD, ⚭ of Yorktown, born 28th July, 1770. Mar. ELIZABETH, dau. of Benjamin Field. | WM. FIELD, ⚭ born and Dec., 1777. Mar. ⚭ ⚭ FAIRCHILD. | MOSES FIELD, ⚭ SUSAN KITTREDGE, of New York, dau. of Honble. born 4th Oct., Samuel Osgood, 1779. mar. at 1st, ELEANOR, dau.of New York Wm. de Forest ; 17th May, 2ndly, Catharine, 1821, died at dau. of Samuel Peekskill, Bradhurst, by whom N.Y., 21st no issue. Oct., 1833. | HICKSON W. FIELD, ⚭ born 17th Oct., 1788. He married 1st, ELEANOR, dau.of Wm. de Forest ; 2ndly, Catharine, dau. of Samuel Bradhurst, by whom no issue. | SEAMAN FIELD, ⚭ of New Or-leans, mar. ELIZA DUBOURG. Left issue. | SARAH FIELD, mar. CALEB HORTON. | PHOEBE FIELD, mar. HENRY FOWLER. | JONAH FIELD, ABIGAIL FIELD, JAMES FIELD, JERUSHA FIELD, SAMUEL FIELD. } Died young and unmarried. |

| MAUNSELL B. FIELD, ⚭ JULIA, born 26th March, dau. of 1821, mar. 7th Jan., Daniel 1846. Assistant Sec- Stanton, retary United States of New Treasury. York. | OSGOOD FIELD, ⚭ KATHARINE ROZANA, born 14th Nov., dau. of Milton Day 1823, mar. in Parker, of Utica, London 7th N.Y. Oct., 1880. | FRANKLIN C. FIELD, mar., 1861, MARY CUNNINGHAM, by whom no issue. | M. AUGUSTUS FIELD, ⚭ FANNY, born 15th April, 1831, dau. of mar. 16th March, Samuel 1854. Bradhurst. | WM. HAZARD FIELD, ⚭ AUGUSTA C., SUSAN M. FIELD, CAROLINE M. FIELD, born 5th Aug., 1833, dau.of Samuel mar. JOHN AU- mar. GEORGE RIGGS. mar. 15th Oct., 1863. Bradhurst. GUSTUS PELL. |

(Under M. Augustus Field) FRANKLIN C. FIELD, mar., 1861, MARY CUNNINGHAM, by whom no issue. 2ndly, ELIZABETH FITCH, in 1879, by whom 1 daughter, LOUISA, born 25th Nov., 1872.

| MAUNSELL B. FIELD, born 21st Oct., 1848. | HICKSON W. FIELD, born 14th July, 1850. | JULIAN FIELD, born 23rd April, 1852. | MARY P. FIELD. | WM. B. OSGOOD FIELD, born 16th Sept., 1870. |

| MARY FIELD. | MAUNSELL B. FIELD, born 1st Nov., 1863. | AUGUSTUS B. FIELD, born 6th Feb., 1866. | THOMAS P. FIELD, born 31st July, 1868. |

can still recall the pleasure it gave his father to see the half-starved applicants have their hunger satisfied.

This was but one instance in many of a career of active benevolence. Often during his lifetime a deserving and needy person had a load of wood deposited at the door when the cold was severe ; or a loaf or two of bread left at the house daily, who never knew the name of the donor, for he was one of the few who "do good by stealth."

His widow, Susan, never recovered from the effects of his loss, and she died in the month of May, 1834, some six or seven months after her husband.

Some further details of the family will be found in Bolton's " History of Westchester, N.Y.," part of which were supplied by the author ; but there are other statements in the book, for which he is not responsible.

ARMS OF THE FAMILY.

HE arms borne by the family of which the author is writing, are what is termed in heraldry "canting," or "armes parlantes," because of their allusion to the name—the garbs or wheatsheaves on the shield being the chief production of the *fields*. Their simplicity is an evidence of their antiquity, apart from the statement in Symonds' diary, that he saw them on monuments of knights of the name of Field in Madeley church, which were of the thirteenth century. It was only during the first half of it that coat armour came into use in England. The most ancient roll of arms there, of which any copy exists, is that of the reign of Henry III., and is supposed by competent authorities to have been made in 1240 to 1245. In this the arms of the Barons de Segrave are given as " sable, three garbs or."

A little later, in the same century, the Earls of Chester assumed as their arms, " azure, three garbs or." Probably the Fields did not adopt their coat until after these two had been used, and were therefore obliged by the laws of heraldry to choose one differing in some respect from those described, and they accordingly selected for theirs the arms on the monuments in Madeley church, " sable, three garbs argent."

These arms, differenced by a chevron, were confirmed to John Field, of East Ardsley, in the manor of Wakefield, in 1558, and it has been stated that they were used by Matthew Field, of Wakefield and London, at about the same time, and are now on an old house at Crofton, at which place several members of this same family resided in the sixteenth and seventeenth centuries.

It was a serious matter at this time for any one to assume a coat to which he was not entitled by right of descent, or of a grant from the College of Arms. The Earl Marshal's Court imposed heavy fines, and sometimes personal confinement on those who violated the laws of heraldry.

The author would remark that the arms assigned to the Fields of Weston in the Hertfordshire Visitation of 1664, are identical with those confirmed to John Field of East Ardsley, and with the crest granted to him in 1558, except that the chevron is "engrailed." The inference from this great resemblance of the two coats is, either that the Hertfordshire family claimed relationship with that of Wakefield manor, but could not prove it ; or else that, being of the same stock, they wished to found a separate branch.

UNIMPORTANT PLACES IN ENGLAND REFERRED TO.

(The distances are approximate.)

Almondbury,	3	miles S.E.	of	Huddersfield.
Ardsley, East,	3	,, N.W.	,,	Wakefield.
Brighouse,	4	,, S.E.	,,	Halifax.
Calverley,	4	,, N.E.	,,	Bradford.
Coley,	3	,, N.E.	,,	Halifax.
Crofton,	3	,, S.	,,	Wakefield.
Cross-stone,	7	,, W.	,,	Halifax.
Hipperholme,	3	,, N.E.	,,	,,
Horbury,	3	,, S.W.	,,	Wakefield.
Horton,	1	,, S.W.	,,	Bradford.
Kirkheaton,	3	,, E.	,,	Huddersfield.
Methley,	5	,, N.E.	,,	Wakefield.
Midgley,	4	,, W.	,,	Halifax.
Newsome.	See Almondbury.			
Normanton,	3	miles N.E.	,,	Wakefield.
Northowram,	2	,, N.E.	,,	Halifax.
Ripponden,	6	,, S.W.	,,	,,
Roystone,	6	,, S.	,,	Wakefield.
Sandal,	2	,, S.	,,	,,
Shelf,	4	,, N.E.	,,	Halifax.
Southowram,	2	,, S.E.	,,	,,

Sowerby,	3 miles	S.W.	of	Halifax.
Thornhill,	5 ,,	S.W.	,,	Wakefield.
Thornton,	3 ,,	W.	,,	Bradford.
Warley,	2 ,,	W.	,,	Halifax.
Woodsome,	3 ,,	S.E.	,,	Huddersfield.

APPENDIX.

ENTRY IN THE COUCHER BOOK OF WHALLEY
ABBEY.

HIS entry is one of ninety-four documents relating to Spotland in the Chartulary. It embraces a conveyance and quitclaim, numbered respectively 62 and 63. The former commences, "Sciunt presentes et futuri quod ego Adam filius Henrici del Feld concessi," etc. The quitclaim begins, "Omnibus hoc presens scriptum visuris vel auditoris Robertus filius Ade filij Henrici del Campo salutem."

The Abbey of Stanlaw received a grant of land at Spotland about the year 1200. The building erected in this neighbourhood by the monks was destroyed by fire in 1289, and they removed to Whalley in 1296.

WILL OF WILLIAM FEILD OF NORTHOUROME.

"In the name of God amen. I Willm Feild of Northourome in the Countie of York clothier thoughe sicke and weake in bodie yet of whole mind and of sound and p̄fect memorie praysed be God for the same. Do this fifteenth day of Julie in the yeare of our Lord God

1619 make ordeyne and declare this my p̃sent Testament conteyninge therein my whole and last will in mañr and forme followinge to witt.

"First and principally I comitt and comend my soul unto the mercifull goodness of Almightie God my creator beseaching his goodness to pardonn all my offences in by and throughe the meritts death and obedience of Jesus Christ his onely sonn my onely Saviour and Redemer for in and by his meritts is my onely hope of salvačon. And my bodie I willingly yield to the Earthe to be buried in such place of X̃stian buriall as it shall please God my endinge to be. And as consĩnge my worldly goods whereof I am possessed my will and minde is that the churche have right duties thereof And such debts as I owe in right and conscience to any p̃sonne or p̃sonns be first answered and paid out of the same. Also I give and bequeath to Susan my wyffe all such interest right and title and terme of years as I have yet to come and expend in one Teñte nowe in the terme or occupation of me the said Wm̃ Feild late of the lands of one I. Bothomley, also my will and minde is that all the Legacies wᶜʰ I owe to all or any of my children be paid out of my whole goods to witt to my daughter Jane x pounds, to Joseph Feild my sonne x pounds to Susan Tenne pounds and to Isabell and Robert one bond of xxx pounds already taken to theire use. Item I give and bequeath to Robert Rawson my sonne in lawe Five shillings All the residue of my goods, cattells, creditts and debts not before given or bequeathed I give and bequeath to George Feild, Jane Feild, Susan Robt and Isabell Feild equally to be divided amongst them. Also I comit the custodie and tuicōn of Robert Feild and Isabell Feild and of theire porcōns to my brother Edward Feild duringe and untill they come to and accomplishe their sevall ages of Twentie and one yeares. And I name ordeyne and appoint the said Edward Feild my brother Executor of this my last will and Testament praying him to be aydinge and assistinge to my wiffe and children as my hope and trust is in him. In witnes whereof to this my p̄sent last will and Testament I putt my hand and seale and publishe and declare it to be my will in the p̄sence of these whose names are subscribed."

Proved 10th Novr 1619.

WILL OF SUSAN FEILD OF NORTHOURAM.

"In the name of God Amen. The four and twentieth day of February in the twentieth year of the Reigne of our Sov̄reigne Lord James by the grace of God Kinge of England Fraunce and Ireland, Defender of the faith &c. And of Scotland the six and Fiftieth and in the yeare of oʳ Lord according to the computacōn of the Church of England of 1622. I Susan Feild of Black Carre wᵗʰin the Dioces of Yorke widowe late wife of Willm Feild late of Northourome deceased being sicke in bodie but of good and p̄fect memory for wᶜʰ I praise Almightie God doe make and ordeigne this my last will and Testamt in manner and forme followinge. And first I give and comend my soule unto the hands of Almightie God assuredly believinge to have free remission of all my sinnes and ev̄lasting life amongst the blessed Stˢ in the Kingdome of heaven through the meritts and passion of my alone Savioʳ and Redeemer Jesus Christ. And I

comitte my body to the earth to be buried at the dis-
cretion of my Execut^{rs} hereafter named   And as touch-
inge the disposition of my worldly goods First my will
and minde is (that my debts and funerall expenses
beinge discharged) I do hereby give devise and bequeath
unto Will͞m Feild my eldest sonne the somme of twelve
pounds of lawfull money of England and unto Alice my
daughter now wife of Robt Rawson of Wrose the some
of five shillings of like lawfull money of England and
no more nor other legacie in regard the said Will͞m and
Alice are already sufficiently p'vided for and p'ferred by
my said late husband deceased their late father.

"Item I do hereby give devise and bequeath unto
George Feild my sonne the some of Twelve pounds of
lawful money of England to be paid unto him in twelve
yeares to witt yearly and ev̈ie yeare the some of Twenty
shillings duringe the terme of Twelve years at the feast
of St. Michaell Th'arch Angell, and the first paym^t
thereof to beginne at the feast of St. Michael th'arch
Angell wch shall fall next after that Joseph Feild my
sonne shall have accomplished his full age of Twenty
one yeares and the same paym^{ts} to be made by my
Executors hereafter named.

"Item my further will and mind is and I do hereby
give devise and bequeath all the residue of my goods
chattells and debts unto the said Joseph Feild my sonne
and unto Robert Feilde my sonne and Jane now wife of
John Mitchell, Susan Feild and Isabell Feild, my three
daughters to be equally divided amongst them.   And I
do hereby make and ordeyne the said John Mitchell and
Joseph Feild Executors of this my last will and Testament.   In witness whereof I the said Susan Feild the

Testatrix have hereunto sett my hand and sealle the day
and yeare above said. These beinge witnesses
" J. MIDGLEY.
" JONAS MITCHELL.
" MATTHEW MITCHELL."

WILL OF JOHN FIELD, THE ASTRONOMER.

" In the name of God Amen the xxviij[th] day of
december a thousand fyve hundreth eyghtie sixe Anno
Regine Dñe ñre Elizabeth Regina vicessimo nono, I
John Feld of Ardeslowe in the Countie of York farmer
sometymes studente in the mathy mathicales sciences,
beinge weake and feble in bodie but of good and p̄fect
memorie laud and prayse be unto Almyghtie God, do
make, ordeyne and declare this my p̄sent testament conteyninge therein my last will in maner and forme followinge, that is to say.

First and principallie I bequeathe and com̄ende my
soule unto Almightie God my Creator and to his dearlie
beloved sonne Jesus Christ my onelie Saviour and
Redemer, in whome and by the merritts of whose most
precious deathe and glorious passion, resurrection and
assencōn I hope and stedfastlie beleve to have full and
cleare remission, p̄done and forgivenes of all my synes
and offences. And my bodie to the earthe to be buried
w[th]in the p̄she churche porche[1] of Ardslowe where I
am now a p̄risheoner.

" Itm I will that all suche debts and somes of money
whatsoever as I shalbe indetted in, or owe of Right by

[1] Jane, widow of John Field, in her will, dated 1609, desires " my
bodie to be buried by my husband John Feild in Ardslaw church porch."

bound obligatorie, bill or conscience unto any p̄sone or p̄sons at the tyme of my decease shalbe well and trulie answered, satisfied and paid by my executrix hereafter named.

" Itm whereas I do stand bound unto John Franklyne of little chart in the Countie of Kent, esquier, by my deed obligatorie in the some of two, or three hundrethe pounds wth condicŏn that yf God do calle me out of the world before my wyfe Jane Feild, that then I shall leave her the said Jane worthe the some of one hundrethe poundes at the least in money plait, houschold stufe or other chattalles as by the condicŏn of the said obligacŏn mor at large yet dothe and shall appeare. In consideracŏn whereof as well in p̄formance of the same condicŏn of the same obligacŏn as also for divers other good causes and consideracŏns me nowe movinge. I do give unto the said Jane Feild my wife my whole intrest title and farmehold lease or leases and terme of yeares wch I now have, or shall have hereafter of my farmehold wherein I nowe dwell. And the water corne mylne belonginge to the same, wth all the houses buyld-inges, lands, tenements, p̄fytts and hereditaments what-soever wth all and singular their appurtenances to the same belonginge, or in any wyse app̄teyninge, as I nowe the said John Feild enjoyeth the same wth the moytie or one half of all my moveable goodes, as oxen, kyne, yonge beastes, cattalles, horses, meares, colts and calves and the moytie, or one halfe of all my said moveable goodes, as quicke or dead whatsoever. And also the moytie or one halfe of all my corne nowe in the barne and growinge on the ground nowe sowne, wth the moytie of my hay. Also I give unto her all my goodes wthin my bed Chamber wherein I nowe lye, wth all household stufe and furnitur wthin the same Chamber to her propr use for ever. And the said Jane to have and to hold the said farmehold her naturall lyfe yff the said lease, or leases so long contynewe. And yf yt it fortune her to dye before the ende of the same lease, or leases be expired then my will is that she shall bye her will and testament in writinge, or otherwise disposse the same her intrest and possession of my said farmehold to some such one of my child, or children as to her wisdome shall best be licked of.

"Itm I do gyve to James Feild and Martyne Feild my two yongest sonnes all my plate and Jewelles of gould and sylver equallie to be divided betwixt them wth eyther of them a bedstead wth the furnitur, havinge a fetherbed, blanketts, sheets, and counterpayntes to the same.

" Itm I do gyve unto fyve hundrethe poure folkes peny dole, and dynynge all my poure neighboures, the day of my buriall as shortlie after as may be.

" Itm I do give to all my god children twelve pence apece at my wyfes discrecon.

" Itm I do give to my cosine Nowell and Xpofer his sonne some cott or dublatt at my wyfes discrecon.

" Itm to Willm Medley some hose or cott at her discrecon.

"Itm I do give to my gossoppe Willm Shereley and Rowland of the newe pke my huntinge horne wth the rest pteyninge to y^t, wth an Inglishe booke at my wyfes discrecon.

" Itm I do give to my maid Alice Butler and to my man John Hill, yf he please and be obedient and

P

serviceable to my wyfe, attendinge my švice trulie, some such like consideraĉon and remembrance as shall seame good to my wyfe's discreĉon.

" Iĩm I do give to my disalyall and loose lyved sonne Richard Feild one sylver spoone in full payment and satisfaĉon of his child's porĉon wᵗʰ wᶜʰ yf he be not satisfied I will he lose the benefytt of the same.

" The Rest and Residue of all my goodes whatsoever, my debts paid and my funerall expences discharged, I give and bequeath the residue to my eight children, to be bestowed upon them equallie at the discreĉon of my wyfe at such tymes and sessons as they shalbe thought sufficient by their good mother to order and disposse the same with the consent of my suƥvisors of this my last will and testament hereafter to be named.

" Iĩm I do ordeyne and appoynt the said Jane Feild my true and lawfull wyfe to be my sole executrix of this my last will and testament and do nomĩate for my suƥvisoures Roberte Greenwood, gentleman, and Roberte Abbott of Bentley, tanner, wᵗʰ Mr. Wᵐ Dyneley of Swillington to be suƥvisours of this my said last will and testament, prayinge them and everie of them to ƥforme the speciall trust I have reposed in them, to see the same executed accordinge to my conscience and my true meanynge of the same.

" In witnes whereof I the said John Feild to this my ƥsent last will and testament have sett my hand and seale the day and yeare above written.

" These beinge witnesses and sealed and delĩved in the ƥsence of me John Naler, John Adamsone."

Proved May 3, 1587.

CAPTAIN JOHN UNDERHILL.

It has been truly said of Captain John Underhill, that he did more to pave the way for civilization, than any one in our early colonial history. He took a prominent, and, almost always, the leading part, in all the Indian wars of his time; [1] freely exposing himself in hand-to-hand encounters with the natives.

Captain Underhill had seen much service in the Netherlands, in the wars of that country against Spain, before he was selected there in 1630, to drill and command the Boston militia. Probably no man of his time in the American colonies had taken part in so much fighting; notwithstanding which, he became in his later years, a respected and sincere member of the peace-loving Society of Friends.

But little is known of his career in the Low Countries; but he must have borne a good reputation there, and been a man of proved skill and bravery in warfare, or he would never have been chosen for the position he held later in the Massachusetts Colony.

The author is disposed to place the year of his birth as about 1600, and if so, he was in the prime of life when he came to New England in 1630.

It is most unlikely that he should have been born much before the commencement of the century, as he had a posthumous son in 1672.

He probably married his first wife in the Netherlands and brought her with him to New England. Hubbard

---

[1] An instance of this will be found in his " History of the Pequot War," published in England in 1638.

says, in reference to Underhill taking service under the
Government of New Amsterdam,—" he speaking the
Dutch tongue very well, and his wife a Dutch woman."
Her name was Helena, and she joined the church
December 15th, 1633. She is again referred to in the
church records on the " 22ᵈ 6ᵗʰ mo.," 1641, when the
entry reads, " brother John Underhill and sister Helena,
his wife." The writer supposes that she is the wife of
whose illness he speaks, in a letter to John Winthrop,
written in 1656, and that she died not long after. He
married, secondly, Elizabeth, daughter of Robert Feake,
of Watertown and Flushing, sister of Hannah, who married John Bowne. Probably the Captain's marriage
took place in 1658, or early in 1659, as their oldest child,
Deborah, was born, according to the Flushing records,
" 29ᵗʰ 9ᵗʰ mo. 1659."

Captain Underhill died at his place, which he called
"Killingworth," at Matinecock, Oyster Bay, Long
Island, on the 21st 7th month, 1671. He was descended
from an old Warwickshire family, which came there
from Wolverhampton. Their arms were, Argent, a
chevron sable between three trefoils slipped vert, crest,
on a mount (hill), a hind lodged, or. These arms were
on Captain Underhill's seal, of which several impressions
exist attached to deeds, letters, etc. At one time,
the Underhills owned over a dozen manors in Warwickshire, and some of the readers may remember that it was
William Underhill, a member of this family, who sold
New Place at Stratford-on-Avon to Shakespere, in the
Easter term of 1597.

In a book called " The Algerine Captive," by Dr.
Updike Underhill, a descendant of the Captain, published

in 1797, there is a curious anecdote, traditional in the family, that the latter took dispatches to England from Leicester, then in the Netherlands, and that these were wrapped in lead, so that in the event of the vessel in which the bearer of them sailed, being in danger of capture by a Spanish cruiser, they could be thrown overboard and would sink.

Considering the light tone of the book, the writer attached no importance to this story ; but it was curiously confirmed, when " the Leicester Correspondence," which had been hidden from the world till then, was published by the Camden Society. Secretary Walsingham, in December, 1585, wrote to the Earl of Leicester, then in the Low Countries, acknowledging the receipt of dispatches from him, sent by " your servante[1] Underhill," and on February 7th, 1585-6, the Earl wrote to Walsingham : " This vij of Feby. I receive your letter with a pece of lead in y^t lyke a patern of a booke. I know not what y^t meanes." There has evidently been some confusion in handing down this family anecdote,[2] which seems to have been founded on fact ; one of these errors is in attributing this incident to our Captain Underhill, who was not living in 1585, as his youngest son Daniel was not born till the 2nd mo. 1672 ; but there are good grounds for supposing that all these extracts refer to his father, who was probably a son of Edward

---

[1] The word *servant* had not then the restricted meaning it has now, and did not always signify a menial. A gentleman by birth, if in any way in the service of this great earl, would have been sometimes called his " servant."

[2] The doctor says that his ancestor carried letters from Leicester to Queen Elizabeth, and he gives an amusing account of Underhill's interviews with her majesty.

Underhill "the Hot Gospeller." This Edward, who was born about 1500, inherited from his father Thomas the manor of Huningham, which is about four miles N.E. of Kenilworth. Thomas Underhill was great grandson of William, who was living at Wolverhampton in 1423. Edward Underhill distinguished himself at the siege of Boulogne in 1542, and as a reward for his bravery he was made a member of the band of " Gentlemen Pensioners," whose duty was to guard the person of the sovereign.

He had been rather wild in his youth, or in the words of one writer, a "man of pleasure," but being converted to the reformed religion, he became very zealous for the new faith, and was nicknamed, in consequence, "the Hot Gospeller." There is a curious anecdote about him in connection with Lady Jane Grey in " Bibliotheca Britannica." The poor Queen was dethroned on the day when his eldest son, Guilford, was christened, for whom she was godmother, and who was named, by her request, after her husband. Many particulars of him and his eventful career will be found in Fox's " Acts and Monuments of the Church," Strype's " Ecclesiastical Memorials," " Machyn's Diary," and other works relating to his time.

In the latter part of his life, he retired to Huningham, and was living there at the time of the Herald's visitation of Warwickshire in 1563. He is said to have died " at a good old age." He married Joan, daughter of Thomas Perryns, of London. His eldest son, Guilford, died in infancy. He had also Edward, baptized 1556, and Henry, baptized 1561. When the Earl of Leicester was authorized in 1585 to raise 500 of his friends and neigh-

bours to accompany him to the Netherlands and assist
the Dutch in their wars against the Spaniards, nothing
is more probable than that one of these two young men
should have joined his standard, and that he was the
bearer of the dispatches which were wrapped in lead. No
one can read the story of Edward, " the Hot Gospeller,"
and that of Captain John Underhill, without being
struck with the great resemblance in their lives and
characters. Both were courageous soldiers, and had
been rather gay in the earlier part of their career; but
afterwards became sincerely religious.

But perhaps the strongest piece of evidence tending to
show Captain Underhill's descent from " the Hot Gospeller," is that he named his place at Oyster Bay, where
he passed the latter part of his life and died,[1] " Killingworth," which was the common name of " Kenilworth "
in his day ; doubtless, in remembrance of the splendid
castle which was near the home of his father and grandfather and, doubtless, of himself in his youth.

Captain Underhill died, as has been said, in 1671.
His wife Elizabeth survived him, but was no longer
living on November 4th, 1675, when administration on
the estate was granted to John Underhill, the eldest son
of the Captain.

This John Underhill married Mary, daughter of
Matthew Prior, by whom he had a daughter Hannah,
who married Thomas Bowne. They had a son Daniel,
who married Sarah, daughter of Samuel Stringham, by
whom he had Maria Bowne, grandmother of the
author.

---

[1] See Camden's " Britannia," article Warwickshire.

THE BOUNDARIES OF FLUSHING IN THE PATENT OF 1645.

" Upon the north side of Long Island to begin at y[e] westward part thereof at the mouth of a creake upon y[e] East River now commonly called and known by the name of Flushing creeke and so to runne Eastward as far as Matthew Garretson's Bay, together with a neck of land commonly called Tew's neck being bounded on the Westward part thereof with the land granted to Mr Francis Doughty and associates and on the Eastward part thereof with y[e] land granted to y[e] plantation and towne of Hempstede and so to runne in two direct lines unto y[e] south side of y[e] said Island."

JOHN BOWNE.

We learn from the journal of John Bowne, which is still preserved, that he was baptized at Matlock, in Derbyshire, March 9th, 1627, and his father, Thomas, on May 25th, 1595, at the same place.

They left England together in 1649, and arrived at Boston the same year. Not long after they both came to Flushing, where John Bowne married Hannah, daughter of Robert Feake of that place, and previously of Watertown, Mass., on May 7th, 1656. Hannah Bowne became acquainted with some members of the Society of Friends, which resulted in her joining it. Her husband afterwards attended one of their meetings from curiosity, and was so struck by the beauty and simplicity of their worship that he also became a Friend, and invited the members to assemble for their devotions at his house. He was soon complained of for permitting these assemblies under his roof, and afterwards arrested by the Dutch authorities of New Amsterdam, who put him in a dungeon, where he was allowed nothing to subsist on but bread and water. Not long after, he was sent, a prisoner, to Holland, but the Directors there of the West India Company, more tolerant than the Government of New Amsterdam, immediately released him, and in a dispatch dated April 16th, 1663, reprimanded Governor Stuyvesant and the council for their arbitrary conduct.

John Bowne left Amsterdam during the 4th month of this same year, and after a visit to England, and a journey to the West Indies, returned to his home at Flushing, where he arrived on the 30th of 1st month, 1664.

His wife, Hannah, who had received " the gift of the ministry," sailed from New York for England on the 24th of 3d month, 1675, on a religious visit; her husband remaining at home; but he joined her in London on the 13th of 11th month, 1676.

She had a violent attack of fever there the following year, which caused her death.

It is recorded in the register of Friends at Devonshire House, London, as having occurred on the 31st of 11th month, 1677, and the entry adds "age about 40."

Her husband delivered a most touching discourse at her funeral, a copy of which is preserved at the old Bownehouse.

During John Bowne's absence from Flushing, his father, Thomas, died there, according to the Friends'

Q

register on the 18th of 7th month, 1677, which adds, "aged upwards of 82."

John Bowne married his second wife, Hannah Bickerstaffe, at Flushing, in 1679. She died in 1690, and in 1693 he was married for the third time to Mary Cock.

He died not long after, viz., on the 20th of 10th month, 1695, "aged about 68," according to the register. After the notice in it of his death, it says, "He did freely expose himself his houses and estate to the service of Truth," and further on, "He also suffered very much for the Truth's sake."

A letter of Captain John Underhill to John Winthrop, Junior, will be found in the publications of the Massachusetts Historical Society, 4th series, vol. 7, which speaks of John Bowne and his first wife, Hannah Feake. It is dated Southold (Long Island), 12th April, 1656. After mentioning his wife's illness, the writer says, "I ware lateli at Flushing. Hannah Feke is to be married to a verie genticle young man of good abilitie of a loveli fetture and good behayiour."

John Bowne says in his diary, that he and his father, Thomas, were baptized at Matlock, and under date of 7th 1st month, 1663, when he was on his way through England to Holland, he notes down in the same, "At night I came to Matlock to the Lintree." The Rev. W. R. Melville, rector of Matlock, wrote to the author in 1873, "Lintree, or Limetree, was a house. There is still a lane here called Lime Tree lane, and a house called Lime Tree house; but the old building known by that name no longer exists." "Glover's Guide to the Peak," published in 1830, says: "At Matlock Bank .is a venerable lime tree, said to be the same which is mentioned in some writings more than 600 years old."

Among the wills in the Probate Court at Lichfield is that of "Anthonie Bowne of the Lime Tree in the psh of Matlock, yeoman," dated December 1st, 1619. After desiring to be buried in Matlock church, he makes bequests to his grandchild Adam, son of Anthony Woolley, and to Adam's sister Elizabeth; to son Ralph Bowne, and to "my wife Ales Bowne," whom he appoints executrix, together with his youngest son, Thomas Bowne.

Administration on the effects of his widow, who is described in the record as "Alice Bowne, late of the Lyntree near Matlocke," was granted, September 12th, 1634, to "John Bowne of Matlocke, yeoman, son of the deceased."

The author thinks that there is hardly a doubt but that the "youngest son Thomas Bowne," of Anthony's will, was the person of that name who sailed for America in 1649, accompanied by his son John.

Thomas Bowne of Flushing named in his will, which was made in 1675, his brother John, who was in all probability the administrator on the effects of Alice Bowne in 1634, and who, doubtless, remained at "the Lyntree," so that when John, the emigrant, wrote in his diary in 1663, "at night I came to Matlock to the Lintree," he was visiting his uncle.

The Matlock registers do not commence till 1637. They contain an entry in 1644 of the baptism of "Mary daughter of John Bowne of Lintree."

The name of the family was sometimes written Boun, and there are grounds for supposing that it was originally Bohun, which is pronounced as if it were spelt "Boon."

Whether the Matlock family was descended from Humphrey de Bohun—one of the most famous companions of the Conqueror, and Humphrey's descendants, the Earls of Hereford, the author cannot say ; but he would mention a matter which seems to point that way. In the College of Arms, and also in Thoroton's "Antiquities of Nottinghamshire," written in 1677, is a pedigree of Bowne of Bakewell,[1] Derbyshire, beginning with Robert Bowne, whose son Richard was of Bakewell 22nd Henry VI. (1444). The arms assigned to this family are, "azure, on a bend argent cottised or, between 6 lions rampant or, 3 escallops gules," while those of the great family of Bohun are, "azure, a bend argent cottised and between 6 lioncels or." As already stated, John Bowne's daughter, Hannah, married Benjamin Field. This couple were great grandparents of the writer's father. John Bowne's son, Samuel, by his first wife, born in 1667, married Mary Beckett, and they had a son, Thomas, who married Hannah, daughter of John, and granddaughter of Captain John Underhill. There was issue of this last marriage a son, Daniel Bowne, by whose wife Sarah, daughter of Samuel Stringham, he had a daughter Maria, grandmother of the writer on his mother's side. It results from this, that his parents were fourth and fifth cousins, through their descent from John Bowne, and yet they were ignorant of any relationship between them, when they married.

---

[1] Bakewell is only about ten miles from Matlock.

ROBERT FEAKE, FEEKE, OR FEAKS.

Robert Feake was at Watertown, Mass., as early as 1630, and represented that town in the Massachusetts Court of Deputies many years. He came to Flushing in 1650, and died in 1668 at an advanced age. He married Elizabeth, daughter of Thomas Fones, of London, and Anne, his wife, who was daughter of Adam Winthrop, of Groton, Suffolk, and sister of John Winthrop, Governor of the Massachusetts colony.

Elizabeth Fones was first married to her cousin Henry Winthrop, son of the Governor, who was drowned at Salem about a year after. A little later she became the wife of Robert Feake, by whom she had a daughter Hannah, who married John Bowne of Flushing, and another, Elizabeth, the second wife of Captain John Underhill. Robert Feake survived his wife Elizabeth, and married again ; for administration on his estate was granted to his widow, *Sarah*, the 19th June, 1669, Mount Feake, at Waltham, was named after this Robert.

HANNAH BURLING.

Hannah Burling, daughter of William and Rebecca Burling, of Flushing, was born the 16th of 10th month, 1713, and married there to Anthony Field, the 13th day of 6th month, 1730; at which time she had not completed her seventeenth year.

Her father, William, third child of Edward and Grace Burling, was born in England the 26th 10th month,

1678. This Edward arrived in America shortly after, as appears by an entry of the births of his seven children in the Flushing register of the Friends, where it is stated that three were born in England and four in America. This enables us to fix the date of his emigration at from 1678 to 1681 inclusive, as his fourth child was born in the last-named year, and was three years younger than the third.

Rebecca Burling, the mother of Hannah Field, died the 2nd of 2nd month, 1729. The author does not know her maiden name, but would mention two circumstances which may be of some help in ascertaining it. Her husband William, in his will, which is recorded at the Surrogate's Office, New York, gives to "my daughter Hannah Field," besides a bequest of money, "a chest which was her mother's marked R.S.," and to Sarah Bloodgood, another daughter by his wife Rebecca, "a silver porringer which was their mother's, marked E.S.M."

William Burling married a second wife, Mary, who survived him, and is mentioned in his will.

He died, according to the Friends' register of Flushing, the 10th day of 8th month, 1743. (The last figure is indistinct.) The following is the entry of his widow's death: "Mary Burling, widow of Wiliam Burling, dyed 25th day 8th mo., 1747."

Her will, also at New York, was dated September 4th, 1746.

This family gave the name to "Burling Slip," New York, having obtained a grant of land in the vicinity in 1737.

Watson says, in his "Annals of New York," "Burling Slip was so called after a respectable family of that name, living at the corner of Smith's Vly (now Pearl Street), and Golden Hill."

Probably the family referred to was that of Edward Burling, eldest brother of William, whose will, dated February 14th, 1744, describes him as "Merchant of New York."

WILLIAM HAZARD.

The Hazard family of Rhode Island has been a numerous one, and it has always held a prominent position in that State.

William Hazard, the father of Lydia Field, was son of Caleb Hazard and Abigail Gardner, great granddaughter of Joseph Gardner, one of the first settlers of Rhode Island. Caleb Hazard was son of George, grandson of Robert, and great grandson of Thomas Hazard, who was in Rhode Island about the time of its settlement by Roger Williams.

This Thomas is supposed to be the person of that name, who was admitted freeman at the Massachusetts General Court, May 25th, 1636, and his son Robert is said to have been four years old, when they arrived in America, probably not long before this date.

The ancestry of Thomas Hazard has not been satisfactorily traced, as far as the author knows. Some accounts say that he came from Wales; but this statement does not seem to rest on any solid foundation, and the writer is disposed to think that he belonged to the family of Lyme Regis, Dorsetshire. It is also said, that he was a ship builder—a branch of industry which flourished at the place named, at the time of his emigration.

Unfortunately the parish registers of Lyme contain but one entry between 1572 and 1649. The family of this town were descended from a John Hazard, or Hassard, lord of the manor of Seaton in 1469; which place is about seven miles from Lyme. John Hazard, born in 1531, was chosen seven times mayor of Lyme, and was its representative in three Parliaments. His son Robert, born in 1582, was also returned member for Lyme in 1614 and 1620.

William Hazard, the father of Lydia Field, married Phœbe, daughter of Captain John Hull, who commanded a ship usually trading between Newport, R.I., and England. Sir Charles Wager was apprenticed to him when a lad, and an anecdote of these two will be found in the "New England Historical and Genealogical Register" of April, 1877.

Captain Hull married, in London, Alice Tiddeman, on the 23rd of 8th month, 1684. He was the son of Tristram Hull of Barnstable, Mass., and Blanche, his wife, and born in March, 1654. Tristram's father was the Rev. Joseph Hull, who was born in 1595, matriculated at St. Mary's Hall, Oxford, May 22nd, 1612, and took his B.A. degree there November 14th, 1614.

He was instituted to the rectory of North Leigh, Devon, April 4th, 1621, and resigned this living in 1632, probably from conscientious motives. He sailed from Weymouth for New England on March 20th, 1635, with his wife Agnes, seven children, and three servants; his third child, Tristram, being three years old at the time.

` The Rev. Joseph Hull is described in the passenger list of the vessel in which he embarked, as " of Somerset-shire." He was minister in two or three different places after his arrival in America, the last of which was the Isle of Shoals, Maine, where he died, a poor man, on November 19th, 1665.

Savage mentions, as a touching circumstance, that, although the value of his whole estate was but £52 5s. 5d., "£10 of it is put down for books."

HICKSON W. FIELD.

Hickson W. Field came to New York at about the age of eighteen, and entered the counting house of Bradhurst and Field, of which firm his brother, Moses, was a partner.

After acquiring some commercial experience, he made a voyage to Guadaloupe, and embarked on his return in the ship " Washington," which was captured by the British sloop of war, " Hippomines," and taken to Antigua, where she was released after fifty days' deten-tion, as no French goods were found on board.

Mr. Field spent the following winter at Charleston, and was present later at the inauguration of President Madison on March 4th, 1809.

Not long after his return to New York, he sailed from there for Amsterdam, and passed the British fleet in the Scheldt, which was attempting to intercept the French.

His vessel, the " Dean," passed unnoticed between two lines of battle ships, and anchored in the Texel

R

roads; but was driven ashore in a violent gale and condemned.

Her cargo af sugar and coffee was seized by the Government of Holland, whose throne was then occupied by Louis Buonaparte.

In 1831 Mr. Field recovered damages from France for this seizure, under the treaty made with that country by the United States during Jackson's Presidency.

From Amsterdam, Mr. Field visited successively London, Cadiz, Palermo, and New York. He returned to London from the last place and opened a commission-house there, which he gave up shortly after, on the passing of the Non-importation Act, and left England for Holland, accompanied by Mr. George Astor, a nephew of John Jacob, the founder of the New York family of the name.

They landed at the mouth of the Elbe, in a smuggling boat, in defiance of a French prohibition, and by doing so, incurred the penalty of death.

On the approach of a sentinel, they had to lie down to avoid detection, and after several narrow escapes, they reached Oldenburg, where their passports were " visés " for Bremen. They sent them to the Commissary of Justice on their arrival at Neustadt, and were summoned by him to attend in person.

Mr. Field, who spoke German, underwent a long examination, in the course of which he stated that he had corresponded with Meyer and Co., of Bremen, so Mr. Meyer was sent for; who not only identified Mr. Field, but also became his bail.

After a visit to Copenhagen, Mr. Field returned to

America, where he arrived just before war broke out with Great Britain, whereupon he joined a well-known New York company called the "Iron Greys," and served with this corps during hostilities.

On their cessation, he established a commercial house, from which he retired many years before his death.

He married in 1818, Eleanor Kingsland, daughter of William de Forest. His wife died at an early age after giving birth to three children, one of whom died in infancy. He married, secondly, Catharine, daughter of Samuel Bradhurst and widow of John McKesson. She died at Nice in 1868, leaving no issue.

Mr. Field died at Rome February 12th, 1873. By his first wife he left a son, Hickson W., who married Mary Elizabeth, daughter of John M. Bradhurst, and a daughter, Eleanor Kingsland, wife of the Hon. John Jay.

THE HON. SAMUEL OSGOOD.

Samuel Osgood, third child of Peter Osgood and Sarah, daughter of Benjamin Johnson, was born at Andover, Mass., February 3rd, 1747-8, on the estate which had belonged to his family since the settlement of this town in or about 1642.

Peter Osgood was son of Timothy and grandson of another Timothy, who married Deborah Poor.

The last-named Timothy was son of John Osgood and Mary Clements, or Clemence, and grandson of John Osgood of Wherwell,[1] near Andover, England, and of Andover, Mass.

[1] Pronounced as if spelt "Herrell."

The author cannot say how long the family had resided in the neighbourhood of the Hampshire town before John Osgood removed to New England; but they were certainly there for more than a century prior to his departure, and mostly living in the parishes of Wherwell, Upper and Nether Wallop.

Unfortunately, many of the wills of Osgoods, named in the Calendar of the Bishop's Court, Winchester, are missing. Fruitless searches were made for the author, for those of Peter Osgood, of Wallop, 1534, Richard of same place, 1543, and several others.

The parish registers of Upper Wallop begin: burials, 1538; marriages, 1540; baptisms, 1684. Those of Nether Wallop commence in 1631, and of Wherwell in 1633. The entries relating to Osgoods in the Upper Wallop registers are numerous, the first being the burial of John Osgood in 1542.

Robert Osgood, of Cottingworth, in the parish of Wherwell, made his will August 25th, 1630, and names in it his sons Stephen and Robert, and daughters Mary and Dorcas. John Osgood is named in a list of debtors, as owing the testator £4 9s. This John may have been the emigrant, and also a son of Robert, the maker of the will.

John Osgood apparently sailed for New England in the ship "Confidence" on April 14th, 1638. In her passenger list, preserved at the Public Record Office, London, is the following: "Sara Osgood of Herrell, spinst[r] and 4 children, William Osgood, William Jones, children under xj years. Margery Parke, servant."

William Jones was, in all probability, John Osgood, who was leaving in disguise, being a subsidy man, and to aid him in this subterfuge, his wife described herself as "spinster." At this period, it was a very difficult matter for anyone who was liable for the payment of subsidies to obtain permission to go abroad; the government having great need of money.

We know from a letter of Dr. Stanley, then head master of Winchester School, in the Public Record Office, that he had applied to the Secretary of State unsuccessfully, for a pass for New England, for John Osgood, shortly before the sailing of the " Confidence." Sara was undoubtedly the wife of the emigrant. This is shown by the baptismal entry of their daughter, Elizabeth, in the Wherwell registers (the only one of their children named in it), which reads as follows: " 1636, Elizabeth Osegood the daughter of John Osegood was baptized the 14ᵗʰ of November and *Sarah his wife*" ; and also by the husband's will, dated April 12th, 1650, in which he names his wife Sarah. This daughter is mentioned in her father's will, and she married John Browne on October 12th, 1659. William Osgood may have been the eldest child of John and Sarah, and over eleven years of age in 1638; or the person of that name, who was a proprietor at Salisbury in 1640, and who was born, by some accounts, in 1609. This last could not have been a son of John, whose birth took place in 1595, as he states in his will. John Osgood settled first at Newbury, and was admitted freeman by the Massachusetts General Court, the 22nd of May, 1639. He did not remain there long, as he was at Andover before 1644.

The Hon. Samuel Osgood entered Harvard College in 1766, and, after the usual course, graduated there.

In 1774 the inhabitants of Andover appointed him

their delegate to Congress. Before the war broke out
he had been for some time in command of a company
of " minute men " at Andover, and he says in an auto-
biographical sketch, that he marched with them to
Lexington on the memorable 19th of April, 1775, and
took part in the running fight with the British troops,
pursuing them as far as Cambridge. His conduct on
this occasion probably brought him to the notice of
General Ward, the first commander-in-chief of the
American forces, who appointed him one of his aides-de-
camp, with the rank of colonel. Not long after, the
town of Andover chose him its representative in the
State Congress, and he left the army, notwithstanding
that he was offered the command of a regiment. This
assembly made him one of the members of the Board of
War.

In the spring of 1781, the Legislature sent him as a
delegate to the Congress of the United States, which
position he held till 1784, when he left it, the constitution requiring a rotation in this office every three years.
In 1785, the United States Congress appointed him first
Commissioner of the Treasury, and he continued to hold
this position till 1789, when the departments were re-
arranged under the new constitution.

As bonds were required from the holder of this office
to the amount of $100,000 (which was a very large
sum in those days), for the faithful performance of its
duties, Osgood was on the point of declining it, when it
was offered to him, rather than ask his friends to be his
security, when the legislature of Massachusetts decided,
by a resolution of both houses, that this state would be
responsible for him.

Not long after his retirement from the Treasury department, General Washington—with whom he had been on terms of intimacy since the commencement of the war—offered him a seat in his cabinet with the office of Postmaster-General, which he accepted and held till 1800, when he resigned, and received a more lucrative appointment; the Supervisorship of the State of New York.

When this office was abolished he was made naval officer of the port of New York, a position which suited his tastes, and enabled him to carry out a long cherished wish to make the city of that name his home, as well as affording him much leisure.

His first wife was Martha Brandon, whom he married January 4th, 1775. She died without issue September 13th, 1778. On May 24th, 1786, he was married to his second wife, Maria, daughter of Daniel Bowne, of Flushing, and widow of Walter Franklin, of Franklin Square, New York. A family anecdote may not be out of place here. When New York was chosen as the seat of government, Washington wrote to Osgood to procure for him there a residence, suitable for the chief of the State. The Franklin mansion, where Osgood's future wife was then residing, was probably the finest dwelling in the city at that time, and although he was a stranger, he called on her to learn if it were possible to obtain the house for the President.

He found Mrs. Franklin surrounded by her three little girls, whom she was teaching their lessons. These children became respectively the wives of Dewitt Clinton, George Clinton, and John Norton.

Mrs. Franklin required time for consideration, and

several interviews took place between her and Osgood, before arrangements were made to give up the mansion to Washington.

Osgood had been greatly impressed by the lady the first time they met, and often spoke in later years of the charming group which presented itself to his eyes as he entered the room. As a result of their interviews, a mutual regard sprang up, which led to their engagement and marriage.

Family tradition says that the sword of the first British officer, who surrendered in the Revolutionary war, was handed by him to Captain Osgood, at the battle of Lexington. If the author's memory serves him, he was a Major Dunbar.

Some of Samuel Osgood's book-plates are in the author's possession. The arms on them are or, three garbs and the crest a demi lion rampant, holding in the paws a garb. The colouring of the garbs and the demi lion is not clear. The author was told in his boyhood, that these arms, worked in tapestry, and brought from England by John Osgood in 1638, were then in the old home of the family at Andover, Mass. Some further particulars of the Osgoods will be found in the " New England Historical and Genealogical Register " for January, 1866.

MAUNSELL BRADHURST FIELD.

Maunsell B. Field entered Yale College in 1837, and graduated in 1841 with the highest honours of his class ; delivering the valedictory on that occasion. He was admitted to the New York bar in 1847, and practised for a few years in connection with the Hon. John Jay.

Not having much taste for law, and being, on the other hand, fond of travel, he gave up the practice of his profession and went abroad.

While in Europe, he was Secretary of Legation for a time in Paris under Judge Mason, and later, President of the American Commission at the Universal Exhibition there in 1855. On this occasion, he received from the Emperor, Louis Napoleon, the ribbon of the Legion of Honour.

After his return to America, he was appointed by President Lincoln, Assistant Secretary of the United States Treasury, a post which he held for some years, but resigned in 1865, as his health broke down under the terrible strain which his duties brought upon him during the war.

Shortly after, he was made one of the collectors of Internal Revenue at New York, but resigned this post after a while, on being offered a district Judgeship there, which offer he accepted.

Judge Field wrote a volume of reminiscences, and a novel called "Adrian," conjointly with his friend, G. P. R. James. He also translated two or three works from the French, of which language he was thoroughly master.

MOSES FIELD.

The average daily number of rations given out at the soup house, which Mr. Field established at the corner of Houston and Mercer Streets, was 2,686. The following obituary notice of him appeared in the "New York American," of October 25th, 1833.

"Died at Peckshill on the 21ˢᵗ inst. Moses Field of this city, aged 53 years. The poor could not have sustained a greater loss in an individual. No man had more enlarged, or persevering benevolence in feeding the hungry, clothing the naked and providing for the sick. His greatest happiness appeared to be to mitigate the sufferings and relieve the wants of the virtuous poor."

Another obituary in the New York "Spectator" of October 24th, 1833, reads as follows:

"It falls to our lot to record the death of Moses Field Esq. of this city; who after a lingering illness expired at Peckshill on the 18ᵗʰ inst. at the age of 53. By this dispensation our fellow citizens have cause to deplore the loss of one of the most useful and philanthropic of their members. The poor among us have especial reason to regret the departure of a friend, whose acts of benevolence have rarely been surpassed in any country. He sympathized in their distresses, and, like another Howard,—not content with taking the height and depth,—the external mensuration of human sorrow—he entered the recesses of misery—ministering to the alleviation both of hunger and pain. It is not easy to do justice to that charity which descends from the house-top to the obscurity of the cellar and the stall, lest it may lose in the lowliness of its dispensation, the gran-deur of it's principle; but it was not for show, or ostenta-tion, that Mr. Field visited the abodes of wretchedness. Substantial relief for human suffering was the end he sought for, and the boon he obtained. He founded our soup establishments at a period of unexampled destitution, and he was an efficient and active co-operator in establishing those Dispensaries in our city, that have contributed so much to softening the pains, calamities, and accidents that flesh is heir to.

"In every labour of beneficence he was among the foremost; not merely by contributions from his purse; but by his personal efforts and the higher authority of example.

"In all our institutions for aiding the poorer classes he was prominent, and in the bestowment of *direct* charity he was one of the most efficient and indefatigable of our philanthropists. To say that ' his hand was open as day to melting charity' would be but a common-place remark. It has been a thousand times quoted, but never, perhaps, with greater fidelity than in its application to Mr. Field. His views were liberal and expansive, embracing in their range the great family of man; yet so definite and minute in observance, that his ready ear could catch the wail of individual misery, and his watchful eye discern and his hand be prepared to relieve it, even on its distant approach."

www.ingramcontent.com/pod-product-compliance
Lightning Source LLC
Chambersburg PA
CBHW021118020726
47500CB00003B/815